THE RETURN OF THE DRIFTER

LORI BEASLEY BRADLEY

Published 2020 by Liaison – A Next Chapter Imprint

Edited by Elizabeth N. Love

Cover art by CoverMint

PROLOGUE

Casey was in her pajamas and ready for bed as the introduction theme for her father's favorite western, *The Drifter*, began to thunder from the old television with its wire rabbit ears bent in the direction to pick up the best signal. Her father came in from the kitchen with a fresh bottle of Pepsi in his hand. Casey frowned up as the man settled into his white faux leather recliner with the cold drink, knowing he wouldn't offer it to any of his offspring. Children in the Casper home were only allowed Kool-Aid and only during daylight hours in the kitchen or outside where they couldn't make a mess. Pepsi was a treat only for adults.

"Now, you kids be quiet while Daddy's show is on," her father snarled as he made himself comfortable, set the Pepsi on the table next to his full ashtray, and lit another cigarette, "or I'll tan your hides with my belt and send you to bed early."

Casey and her younger brothers and sister sat quietly, knowing his threats weren't made in jest. They'd all seen that belt come flying out of the loops at lightning speed and suffered the consequences of interrupting one of their father's favorite shows.

The baby in Casey's bedroom began to cry. "Get your lazy ass up and tend to your little sister, Casey," her father ordered. "Put a bottle in her mouth and shut her up during my show."

Casey got to her feet and plodded into the kitchen to find one of the bottles of breast milk her mother had left in the refrigerator before going to her job at the market up the street. She wouldn't return home until after ten when the store closed, and seven-year-old Casey, as the oldest, was left responsible for feeding and changing baby Clea, now five months old. Casey prayed this would be her mother's last baby. None of her friends at school had to change diapers or get up at two in the morning to feed a little sister or brother, and she didn't think it was fair that she had to do it.

Casey had changed her first diaper at age five when her little brother Kenny had come along, but her mother hadn't been working then and kept the crib in their room. She'd also been breastfeeding, so there had been no bottles for Casey to tend either. Casey had heard her mother talking on the phone about taking a pill now to stop her from getting pregnant again, and she hoped it worked.

The show was almost over by the time Casey fed the baby and got her dirty diaper changed. Her father scowled at her when she returned to the room. "It's about time you got that squalling brat settled down, girl. I could hardly hear my show for the screamin'."

"I don't think Clea liked something mommy ate," she said in a soft voice. "Her belly is upset and her poo stinks." She curled her nose in distaste of the memory of the dirty diaper she'd removed from the fussing baby.

"I hope you rinsed the damned thing good in that diaper pail."

Casey grinned at her younger brother. "I washed Clea's butt good, but not in the diaper pail."

Her father just snorted a reply as he lit another cigarette during a commercial about beer. The man never understood her humor or responded to it positively. Her brother laughed behind his hand and whispered, "He's gonna take his belt to you if you get smart with him, Casey."

"Won't be the first time," she rolled her blue eyes and replied in an equally soft whisper, "and probably won't be the last."

They sat quietly until the final theme music began to play. "I hope you find a man like Tucker to marry someday, Casey." Her father emptied another bottle of Pepsi.

"There aren't cowboys anymore, Daddy," Casey said as she roused little Kenny and sent him toddling toward his room.

"Ain't no cowboy gonna wanna marry silly Casey anyways," Micha said with a grin. "She reads too many books."

Their father sat up in his recliner and folded down the footrest. "Of course there are still cowboys, Casey, and," he said to her brother, "she needs a good, moral man like Tucker Hughes to turn her into a good woman who can take care of a house, tend a garden, and mind her children the way a woman should."

"And I bet she can't learn that in silly books, can she, Daddy?" her brother continued to tease.

"Books have a place, son," her father said with a sour glance at Casey, "but it's in school and not at home where there are too many chores for a woman to tend to."

The talking and movement in the living room woke the

baby, and Casey began to fret again. She made a beeline for the bedroom, went in, and shut the door to tend to one of her womanly chores. Clea's diaper was damp, so she changed it before putting the bottle back into her mouth and holding it in place until the baby's eye's closed and she settled back into sleep.

She made a quick trip across the hall to the bathroom, where she relieved herself for the night and then returned to her dark room to crawl into bed. Casey fell asleep to the sound of the television on the other side of the wall and woke later in the dark after another dream about being chased across a field by yelling Indians on horseback.

I

Another divorce was final, and Casey Miller had run away to her friend Tandy's in rural California north of Palm Springs to take stock of her life—or what was left of it.

They stood in the check-out line of Lucky's Supermarket in Yucca with a cart overflowing with groceries Casey insisted on paying for if Tandy insisted upon cooking for her every night. Their visit had been great so far, but Casey didn't know if she could stomach another meal of the spicy Mexican fare Tandy cooked.

The man ahead of them had just said something to make the cashier laugh, and Casey took her eyes off his shapely behind for the first time. He wore the typical cowboy get-up popular in Yucca and of the old western shows Casey's father had loved to watch. His jeans fit tight, and he had a blue bandana tied around his neck. He even wore a perfectly styled brown cowboy hat and polished leather boots. The only thing out of place was the set of aviator sunglasses on his handsome tanned face with lenses tinted yellow.

"Looks just like his dad, doesn't he?" Tandy whispered into Casey's ear.

Casey studied the man closer as he put his bagged purchases into his cart and Tandy moved them forward in the line. "Who is he and who is his dad?"

"That's Tucker Riley," she said. "His dad is Morgan Riley, the actor who played Tucker Hughes on that show *The Drifter*."

"Oh, wow," Casey said, studying the man closer. "He really does look like him—especially in those clothes."

Tandy pushed the cart forward, and Casey began putting groceries onto the rolling rubber belt for the cashier to scan and bag in white plastic bags. "Hey, Tucker," Tandy called, "since when do you do the grocery shopping?"

The man turned to study the person speaking to him. "Oh, hey, Tandy," he said in reply with a big furrow in his tanned brow. "Ever since Elvira left me high and dry over in LA and I moved back up onto the ranch with Mom and Dad."

"I'm so sorry to hear that, Tucker," Tandy said as Casey continued to empty the cart. "I always thought Elvira was real nice and you two were good together." Casey could tell from her friend's tone she didn't mean a word she said to the man about his wife. "You two ever have kids?"

"No," he said with a shake of his head, "and that was probably a big part of our problem." He chuckled. "That and we mixed about like oil and water."

"Balsamic and extra virgin mixes well with a good shake," Casey said without thinking as the cashier rang up her total and she handed the woman her debit card.

"Excuse me?" Tucker said, glancing at Casey for the first time.

"Just excuse her, Tucker," Tandy said as she inched the cart around Casey and began loading bagged groceries into it. "She's suffering from the just-lost-another-man blues."

Casey scowled at her friend. "Or maybe I'm not suffering at all and I'm ready to throw a post-divorce house party—at your house."

Tandy snorted. "Not at my house, you're not. As I recall the last one went on for about three days and involved several cases of wine."

Casey grinned and winked at Tucker Riley. "And a few bottles of Jack Daniels. You can't forget Jack."

"Boy, ain't that the truth," Tandy said, rubbing at her temples.

"Sounds like you gals know how to throw a party," Tucker said with a grin.

Casey signed her receipt and followed her friend who pushed the cart over to join her friend Tucker.

"I'm Tucker Riley, by the way," he said, offering his hand to Casey.

"And I'm Casey Miller," she said as she took the man's big hand. She noticed it was rough and work-worn. This was no idle California movie star's brat. This man worked for a living. "Are you in the business like your father?"

Tucker rolled his dark brown eyes. "Not hardly," he said, "though Mom and Dad both tried to push me into it when I was younger."

"You've certainly got the looks for it," Casey said, and then her cheeks turned pink with embarrassment. "I hear they're trying to bring Westerns back up here in the desert."

He took off his hat and ran a hand through his thick, auburn curls. "My sister and I are hoping that's the case. If not, we're putting a lot of money into Desert Home for nothing."

"Desert Home?" Tandy asked with her face twisted in confusion. "That broken-down old movie set out in the foothills? I thought the county condemned it years ago and had it torn down."

Tucker nodded. "That's what was gonna happen, but Dad and Mom stepped in and bought it from the Studio." He glanced at Casey and smiled. "It's where they shot their show back in the day."

"Their show?" Casey asked, equally confused.

Tandy giggled. "Tucker's mom played Charity on the show. The dancehall girl who was the sheriff's love interest."

"Oh, yah, right." Casey vaguely remembered a blonde saloon girl from the show who always wore an ostrich feather in her hair.

"She's been my Dad's love interest in real life for almost sixty years now," Tucker said, "and I'd best be gettin' these groceries home to her or she'll tan my hide the way she did when I was a kid." He began to push his cart toward the sliding glass door. "It was sure nice seeing you, Tandy."

"Nice seeing you again, Tucker," Tandy replied as she followed him out into the bright high desert sunshine." If you're back up here on the mountain, you should drop by sometime and we could take the horses out."

"I might just do that," he said with a wink at Casey. "You still make those chicken enchiladas in green chili sauce that are so good?"

"She sure does," Casey chimed in, rubbing her abdomen, "though I think she spikes the damned things with jalapenos more than simple chilis."

Tucker and Tandy both laughed. "Not a fan of the hot stuff?" Tucker asked, grinning.

"I've been here for a week, and I think I've already lost the lining of my esophagus and my stomach. I'm cooking tonight," Casey said as they stopped at her car, "and it's gonna be fried chicken, mashed potatoes, biscuits, and gravy."

Tucker smiled, showing off his even, white teeth. "That sounds good too. I think my mom has meatloaf planned." He turned the cart toward a big, dirty pickup. "But she makes it with hot peppers, lots of onion, and Louisiana hot sauce."

"It was real nice meeting you, Tucker," Casey said as she opened the rear hatch on her car, "but I think I'll pass on your mother's meatloaf."

Tucker laughed. "Why don't you gals come out to Desert Home tomorrow and see what we're doing out there."

"The last time I was out there," Tandy said, "we were in high school and it was just a falling down disaster area infested with black widows and rattlesnakes."

"Then you'll be excited to see how much it's changed," he called to them as he returned his empty cart to the rack with the others.

"Sounds like fun," Casey said as she took her empty cart and began pushing it toward the rack as Tandy got into the car and turned on the ignition to get the air conditioning going.

"See you tomorrow then?" He said almost hopefully as he climbed into the truck and started the engine.

Casey returned to the car and got in. "How far away is this Desert Home place?"

"Out about eight miles west of town," Tandy said. "I hope he's fixed it up because the last time I was out there it was a real wreck. I honestly thought the county had bulldozed it a long time ago."

"Sounds like his family is putting a lot into it to fix it back up."

Tandy shook her blonde head. "It would have taken a small fortune to fix that mess up. As I recall, one of the guys with us put his foot right through the floor of the saloon and all the ceilings leaked." She did a mock shiver. "And there were black widow webs full of spiders hanging everywhere in the buildings."

"I'm sure that was easy to clean up," Casey said, "but you know I'm no fan of spiders."

Tandy chuckled. "I know and I'm no fan of rattlesnakes. When we were walking from the parking area through all the old creosote bushes, you could hear the rattles going off everywhere."

"Well, I'd imagine they'd have cleaned all of that up too."

Tandy turned her head and smiled. "I think Tucker was into you, Casey."

"No, he wasn't," Casey scoffed. "He was just being nice to your friend. I think he was into you."

"My chances with Tucker Riley came and went years ago."

"You guys dated?" Casey asked in surprise. She couldn't remember her friend ever mentioning dating the handsome son of a television star.

"In high school," she said, waving her hand, "before he went off to Vietnam. It was nothing really." She sighed. "Just two kids playing around. He went off to Vietnam and I went off to USC. I met Sam in college, and we got married. Tucker came back and hooked up with that shrew Elvira."

"Seems they were together for a long time."

Tandy snorted. "Elvira probably got tired of waiting for his old man to kick the bucket for the inheritance. I know she screwed everything in pants while they lived out here on the ranch." She shrugged her freckled shoulders. "I shudder to think about what went on in LA. Behind his back."

They turned off the main highway onto the bumpy dirt road leading up to Tandy's house. "So he said he and his sister were working together on this Desert Home thing. Do you know her too?"

Tandy nodded. "And a royal bitch she is too," she said as Casey swerved to avoid another pothole. "They're twins. He's the spitting image of their father, Morgan Riley, and Charity is the spitting image of their mother, Rita Wright, who played his love interest on the show."

"And they named their kids after the characters they played on the television show?" Casey asked with a furrowed brow. "That couldn't have been easy on the kids with the show in syndication for so long."

"I'd imagine they'll use that to their advantage when they get ready to open Desert Home up to the public."

"What do you think their plan is—an amusement park like Disney?"

Tandy shrugged as Casey parked the car in the drive of the adobe house shaded by towering eucalyptus and Aleppo pines. "Probably more of a tourist trap like Tombstone or Old Tucson in Arizona with shops and restaurants. I can't see them doing something with rides and shit unless its stagecoach and pony rides." Tandy grabbed some bags. "I doubt the old man would allow it on the old stage set."

2

Casey rose to find a bright and sunny day with the aroma of fresh-brewed coffee wafting into her bedroom from the kitchen. She dressed in comfortable jeans and a blue tank top that molded itself over her heavy breasts, making her feel like she wasn't the aging woman she was. She ran a comb through her freshly colored auburn hair but decided to forgo makeup today other than a bit of pink lip gloss. She pulled on her worn cowboy boots and made her way into the kitchen where Tandy sat with her shoulder-length blonde hair looking perfect. Casey's friend had worked as a fashion model in her younger days and she always looked perfect no matter the situation.

"You look great this morning," Casey said as she filled a mug from the Mr. Coffee on the counter beside the stove. Tandy noted the dishes from last night's dinner had already been put away and the kitchen looked as perfect as her friend. Casey couldn't remember ever having seen Tandy's house anything but perfect. Dressed in what her friend liked to call desert rat chic. The furniture was old and mismatched but clean with the walls and tables covered in twenty years of desert finds. There were framed photos of Tandy with her late husband Sam on trips to Mexico where they explored ancient ruins together and collected pieces of old pottery they found.

One adobe wall also hung with Tandy's collection of western TV and movie memorabilia, including autographed photos of the cast of *The Drifter* in full costume on the Desert Homesite. There were also photographs of Sam with well-known actors like Clint Eastwood and others he'd worked with as a stuntman on the old Westerns. Sam had injured his back and then become dependent on opioids. He'd died of an overdose in this very room ten years earlier, and Casey didn't know how her friend could bear it.

Tandy walked into the living room with a cup of coffee in her hand and went to stare at the large portrait she'd had painted of her and Sam together in the desert with their dog Skipper, searching for treasures together. "He was a handsome devil, wasn't he," her friend said, running a finger over the face of her late husband.

"Indeed he was," Casey said. "He could have been on the screen with any of those leading men and put them to shame."

"Oh, he was," Tandy said in an almost dreamy voice, "and he took all the hard falls for 'em so they looked good to their fans." She smiled. "He loved to point himself out in all the shows when it looked like the lead falling off his horse or taking a tumble down a rocky hillside."

Casey watched her friend kiss her finger and then touch it to her husband's face. It brought tears to her eyes and she looked away, sipping her hot coffee to give Tandy her moment with Sam. "I know he loved what he did," Casey said, trying to keep tears from choking her voice.

"Yah," Tandy said with a sigh, "right up to the day it took him from me." She joined Casey on the couch. "Are you looking forward to our little trip into the desert today?"

"I am," Casey said, happy to be moving on to another subject. "I've never been to a real movie set before."

"Desert Home was never a movie set unless you count the two follow up *Drifter* movies they did there," Tandy corrected. "It was just a studio stage set for that one show."

"Oh, I see," Casey said. "So, where is this family ranch I heard Tucker mention yesterday?"

"It's about five miles on out from Desert Home. Tucker's mom started raising those little miniature horses years ago. They take them to children's hospitals and places like that to entertain the patients."

Casey reached for her friend's empty cup. "That's pretty cool."

"Tucker lost a little brother to leukemia when he was in grade school and his mom started doing the thing with the horses soon after. His name was Tate like the deputy on the show, and I remember he was a really cute kid."

Casey came back into the room with fresh coffee. "Cancer sucks," she said as she resumed her spot on the couch. "Sounds like his mom found a way to deal with it."

Tandy smiled. "Yah, I guess they make a pretty big deal of it when they roll up on a hospital or nursing home with a dozen of those little horses and them dressed in their western garb. The kids and old folks love it."

"Sounds like it could be a great PR thing for their Desert Home thing as well." She sipped her coffee. "The show is still in syndication on some of those channels that rerun old shows. I think I just caught an episode the other day."

Tandy snorted. "It's probably what that bitch Charity is pinning her hopes on."

Casey furrowed her brow. "I gather you don't like his sister much."

"She's one of those snotty-nosed brats who thought her shit didn't stink because her parents were famous and on television," Tandy snarled.

"She beat you out for a part in a school play or for a guy?" Casey asked with a grin tugging at the corners of her mouth.

"Both," Tandy finally said, grinning at the ridiculousness of the aged grudge. She tipped up her cup and swallowed more coffee. "Well, let's get this show on the road. I need to do a load or two of laundry this afternoon, so we can't spend the whole day dawdling with the rich and famous of Yucca." She reached for Casey's cup. "We taking your car or mine?"

"Just filled mine with gas," Casey said as she gathered up her purse and a straw cowboy hat, "but you're driving. I have no idea how to get to this place."

Casey and Tandy left the house with Tandy at the wheel of Casey's burgundy PT Cruiser. They turned off the highway in Yucca and headed toward Desert Home. The blacktop soon turned to a rough dirt road that bounced them around in the car.

"Pretty country out here," Casey said as she stared out the window at the fields of chaparral and high desert wildflowers blooming amidst spiny Joshua trees.

"And busy," Tandy said with a giggle as she slowed the car for a covey of fat Gambel's quail to cross the road guarding a brood of young ones. Tandy laughed when she saw the roadrunner chasing them. "That big fella better watch out cause I've seen a mama quail peck out the eyes of a roadrunner chasing her young."

Casey watched the quail cross the road, followed by the roadrunner, and laughed along with Tandy. She'd seen mother quail defending their young from roadrunners, and the fights could be vicious. The day was sunny with a soft breeze blowing the Palo Verde trees filled with bright yellow blossoms. She could smell their sweet scent on the breeze through the open window. The high desert was beautiful in spring, and Casey was glad she'd come.

"What's that up ahead there?" Casey asked when she saw an animal stumbling along the side of the dusty road.

"Looks like a big dog or something got hit by a car," Tandy said, studying the animal.

"I don't think so," Casey said. "It doesn't move like a dog."

The car got closer, and Tandy slowed. "It's a horse," Tandy said in surprise. "It's one of the miniatures Tucker's mom raises." She stopped when the little horse stumbled and went down on one of its forelegs. "I think it may have been bit."

Tandy stopped the car, and both of them got out, and went to the animal. Tandy spoke softly to the panting little horse, and it stood quietly, waiting for them to come and attend to it. "Her leg is swollen, and she's having trouble standing up on it."

"Poor baby," Casey said as she stroked the soft black fur on the animal's rump.

"Let's get her into your car," Tandy said, opening the rear passenger side door, "and take her out to Desert Home, where Tucker's brother Chris has a stable."

Casey didn't give any thought about how Tandy knew that and hurried to get into the back seat of her car. Tandy lifted the little horse into the car, and Casey took the shivering animal into her arms, helping it into the car. "It's all right," she whispered in a soothing tone as she held the horse's head against her shoulder.

It kicked its rear legs a few times after the car went into

motion and made soft whimpering noises that broke Casey's heart. "It'll be all right, baby, we're gonna get you home and get you some help." The horse quieted with Casey's soft words as if she understood.

"We'll be there in a few," Tandy said as she swung the car onto the road leading up to Desert Home.

Unfortunately, the motion of the quick turn along with the poison in the horse's system did not agree with her, and she vomited down the front of Casey's chest and arm. "We'd better get there soon," she told her friend, "because she just threw up all over me, and it's turning my stomach as well."

Casey rocked forward when Tandy brought the car to a sudden halt. "I'm gonna run up to the stables and see if I can find someone to help," Tandy said breathlessly as she jumped out of the car and took off toward the wooden barn surrounded by a wooden fence filled with other miniature horses. "It looks like you're home, baby," Casey said as she rolled the window down farther to allow fresh air to enter and ease the bitter aroma of the horse's vomit soaking her tank top and bare arm.

A few minutes later, the door jerked open and a tall man with sandy blond hair took the little horse into his arms. "Looks like you found our little escape artist," he said as he took the whimpering horse into his arms to gently carry her into the barn.

Tandy grinned and tossed Casey a roll of paper towels. "Isn't this more fun than just sitting home in front of the boob tube?"

Casey rolled her eyes as she tore off sheets of the white paper and began to wipe away the foul-smelling goo from her chest and arm as she followed Tandy into the barn. She, in turn, followed Chris with the horse into a stall filled with fresh, clean straw. He inspected the horse's leg.

"Damn," he hissed beneath his breath. "You didn't happen to see the snake that bit her, did you?"

"No," Tandy said. "We just came upon her limping up the side of the road. "Why?"

"It makes a difference in which anti-venom I have to administer." He studied the leg again. "From the size of these fang marks, I'm guessing it was a big Diamondback, though. If it had been a Mohave Green, they would be closer together." He glanced up at the shivering animal. "She'd also be a whole lot sicker," he said as he stood and left the stall. "I'm gonna treat her with the Diamondback anti-venom and hope for the best."

The little horse began to fret and whimper once more, and Casey went to her side, petting her softly. "It's all right, baby," she whispered in a gentle voice. "You're home and Chris is going to take good care of you now." Tears filled her eyes and ran down her cheeks as she tried to comfort the animal. She started to stand when Chris returned with a bag of saline and a large needle, but he motioned for her to stay where she was while he found a vein and inserted the needle to begin treating the horse for her snake bite.

Tucker Riley stuck his head into the stall as Chris was finishing up. "What's going on in here?" he asked with his eyes flitting between his brother, the two women, and the horse.

"These fine ladies found our Baby after she'd been snake bit and brought her back to us," Chris said with a glance at Tandy.

"She gonna be all right?" Tucker asked. "Mom'll be heartbroken if she's not."

Chris shrugged his broad shoulders. "Time'll tell, but she's a strong animal, and I think they got her here before the venom had time to get too far into her system."

"It looks like you got the nasty end of that snakebite,"

Tucker said when he noticed Casey wiping at the green vomit on her shirt and arm. "I think I have a shirt you can wear," he said, "and you can clean up in my camper. Then I'll give you girls the full tour of Desert Home."

Casey continued to whisper soothing words to the little horse. "I think I should stay here with her to keep her calm," Casey said as she brushed away tears from her cheek.

"Go on with Tucker and your friend," Chris said, helping Casey to her feet. "I'm gonna give her a sedative to help her sleep."

3

Casey cleaned up in Tucker's fifth-wheel and put on a fresh t-shirt that was three sizes too large for her but welcome after the smelly, wet tank top.

"You all fresh and clean now?" Tandy asked when Casey returned to the living room with her dirty shirt in a plastic bag.

"Where's our host?" Casey asked when she didn't see Tucker.

"Out cleaning up your car," Tandy said.

"He didn't have to do that," Casey said, embarrassed that the man would see her messy car after she'd driven it from Santa Clarita to Yucca.

"Yes, he did," Tandy said with her nose scrunched up. "That horse puke was foul. Both of us would have been gagging all the way back to the house if it had set in the sun all afternoon with that mess in it."

Casey had to agree. "I suppose you're right there." She asked a question that had been scratching at the back of her mind. "So what's going on between you and Tucker's brother, Tan?"

Tandy jerked her head up with her eyes narrowed. "What gives you the idea there's anything going on between me and Chris?"

Casey grinned. "Oh, I don't know, maybe having known you for over twenty years and recognizing that little dimple in your cheek when you grin at that certain someone."

"Don't be silly, Casey," Tandy said in retort. "I'm a mar—"

"You're a widow," Casey said, cutting off her friend, "and you deserve to have a new love in your life if you've found one."

Tandy ran her hand through her thick blonde hair. "Well, in my bed anyhow," she said with an impish grin.

Casey smiled. "I want to hear all the details. He's certainly built like a brick shit house. How is he hung in the equipment department?"

Tandy's cheeks flushed. "He's strung like a fine instrument."

The door opened, and Tucker walked in with a bag filled with wet paper towels and empty fast-food packaging. "She's all back to good as new," he said and winked at Casey. "You look a lot better, too, though my old t-shirt probably doesn't fit very well."

"It's very comfortable," Casey said with her cheeks flaming. "I'm ready for that tour if you guys are."

Tucker went to the refrigerator and took out three cans of Coke. He gave one each to Tandy and Casey before popping the tab on his and swallowing it down. "It's warm and dry out there today, and it's a long walk from here to the other end of town and back."

They followed him out into the bright sunshine. "I'm parked here behind the main set, which was Miss Charity's Dance Hall if you remember from the show. My sister is planning to turn it into a full-scale restaurant and saloon to feed our hungry and thirsty visitors as well as possibly a wedding venue."

They walked into the building through a back door and saw a bevy of individuals busy at work on the building. "This is really amazing," Casey said. "You could get tons of Steampunk and SASS folks up here in costume for events if they knew it was available."

A woman approached in dusty jeans and a long-sleeved work shirt. "My hopes exactly," she said in a smug tone, eying Casey's attire.

"My sister Charity Riley," Tucker said. "This is Casey Miller, and I think you know Tandy."

Charity snorted. "Who could forget the class tramp?"

Casey grabbed her friend's hand and held it tight to keep her from jumping the officious woman, and Tucker continued as though he hadn't heard his sister's slur. "They've come up to see what we're doing with the place."

"Desert Home never had a brothel," Charity said with her eyes riveted on Tandy. "It was a family show, so if you're looking to franchise a building, you'll need to come up with something more wholesome than you're inclined to, Tandy."

Charity turned and walked away, leaving Casey stunned and Tandy shivering with rage. "That bitch hasn't changed since high school," Tandy spat.

"I gather she doesn't know about you and Chris," Casey asked softly.

"Not on your life."

Tucker cleared his throat. "Please excuse my sister," he said in apology to Tandy. "All of this has her a bit out of sorts."

Casey glanced around the building. "Did she never really watch the show?" Casey asked, pointing up to the top of the stairs, "because all those doors up there on the second floor were where those girls, in short, low-cut dresses hustling drinks, took men to screw and Miss Charity was the damned Madam of the house."

"I suppose I should have my mom talk with her about that," Tucker said with an embarrassed grin.

He took both their arms and led them out into the sunshine again. "At one end of the street is the courthouse and at the other end is the church/schoolhouse." He pointed at each. "And in between, we have all manner of businesses. The Desert House Hotel, which we already have franchised along with the mercantile, the barbershop, and the livery where we have a guy who will be giving blacksmithing demos and making knives and other things he will sell in the storefront."

When they came to one building, Casey stopped. "Oh, I remember Miss Millie's Dress Shoppe," she said. "I loved her and her niece Patty."

"We've been looking for a seamstress to take this building," Tucker said, "but nobody seems interested in putting up the money for the franchise fee or what it would take to get the building up to code."

"Explain this franchise fee you keep mentioning," Casey said as Tucker unlocked the door to the dress shop and they went inside.

"It's like buying into Desert Home," he explained. "The person is buying the right to say they are a Desert Home business owner and no different than buying a McDonald's or Burger King franchise."

Tandy furrowed her brow. "Why not just flat out rent the buildings to people?"

"Because franchisees must adhere to specific guidelines set up by the corporation like building design and the products sold," Casey said. "You can't sell fried bologna sandwiches at a Burger King—only their brand of burger."

"Oh," Tandy said, "so a dressmaker at Miss Millie's would only be able to sell what—dresses they showed on the show way back when?"

Tucker rolled his eyes and smiled at Casey. "She would only be able to sell dresses that would have been worn in that time period. I think the show was set in 1875 or '76."

"Ah," Casey sighed, "the lovely bustle period in our clothing history."

"What?" Tucker said with his brow furrowed.

Tandy giggled. "Casey here is a historical clothing expert. She spent the last twenty years making and selling costumes at Renaissance and Medieval fairs."

"Really?" Tucker said with his eyes wide. "Have you ever done any cowboy period stuff?"

Casey smiled. "I love the nineteenth century. The women's clothes were so much fun with all the ribbons and lace."

"Do you think you could work with this?" he asked, motioning around the dusty building. "Come on and let me show you the rest of the place. The living quarters are back here."

"Living quarters?" Casey said.

"Franchisees are expected to live on-site during the tourist season," he said as he opened a curtain to expose a small kitchen, a space with a long trestle table Casey could see as a wonderful cutting table, and an area meant as a sitting room with a broken down settee and dusty side tables. Tucker opened a door to reveal a porch, and Casey could see the road leading into Desert Home. "Here is the bedroom," he said. The women peeked into a small dark room that probably wouldn't hold much more than a full-size bed and dresser.

"So," Casey asked, "how much is this franchise fee, and what would be expected of me as a franchisee?"

"Are you seriously considering this, Casey?" Tandy asked with her eyes wide.

Casey shrugged. "I gotta do something with my life now that I'm single again and out of the Medieval game now." Her soon to be ex-husband had sold all her stock along with the booth a year ago without discussing it with her first. It was one of the main reasons he was her soon to be ex-husband.

"Well," Tucker said hesitantly, "the fee is seventy-five thousand dollars, and you have to agree to bring the buildings back to what they were in the show."

Tandy gasped. "Damn, Tucker, you don't want much, do you?"

"Hey," he exclaimed, "franchisees at Burger King and all those places have to pay for building their stores to the company's design."

Casey went to inspect a piece of the dusty, peeling wallpaper. "I suppose that makes sense. How much do you think I'd be looking at to accomplish that?"

"You'd need to meet with Frank," Tucker said. "He's our in-house contractor who's taking care of getting Desert Home back into its original state." He smiled at Casey. "I can set that up for you if you want before you make a decision."

Casey nodded her head. "That would probably be a good idea. I should know what I'm getting into here."

Tandy went to a set of stairs and craned her head to look up. "Where do these go?"

"It's a small bedroom or probably more practical as a storage area." Tucker mounted the creaky stairs, and the women followed him up. He opened the door and flipped on a light.

Casey gasped at the webs and spiders in the small, dark space. "I'm not going in there until there's been an exterminator here." She turned and ran back down the stairs.

"She's the original arachnophobe," Casey heard Tandy telling Tucker and laughing.

"I'll call and have Terminix out here tomorrow if you're serious about the franchise, Miss Miller," Tucker said when they came back down the stairs. "Would you happen to have any examples of your work you could show me?"

"All my stuff is still in storage back in Santa Clarita," Casey said.

Tandy took out her phone. "I got you covered, girl." She began bringing up photos to show to Tucker. She turned to Casey. "Do you have anything on your phone like pictures of your booth and how people filled it up as soon as you opened the damned thing every day?"

Casey took out her phone and brought up photos to share with Tandy and Tucker. "This is all Medieval stuff," she said apologetically, "but I think I have one of myself in a Steampunk outfit I made to wear to a function a year or so ago."

Casey found the photo of herself in the teel-and-white striped outfit made up of a bodice with mutton sleeves and a flounced skirt of the same fabric over a solid teel poplin underskirt. The bodice fastened with white frogs, and she'd topped it off with a white felt bowler hat decked out with peacock and ostrich feathers, white lace gloves, and white lace-up granny boots. "Here it is," she said and handed the phone to Tucker with Tandy crowding in close to have a look.

"How did I never see that work of art?" Tandy asked.

"It was a one-time thing," she said with a shrug. "Some of my medieval friends were getting into Steampunk and invited me to one of their dinners at the Old Spaghetti Factory."

Tucker smiled. "I think you'll make a fine fit here at Miss Millie's, Casey."

"Well, let me think about it while you get rid of those harbingers of death in the room upstairs," Casey said with a grin.

4

Dinner that night at Tandy's was tense. Casey saw a great opportunity in Desert Home, but she was having a difficult time wrapping her head around putting up that much money for an untested venture.

"You've got the money, right?" Tandy asked as she slid a tortilla warmer across the table toward Casey. "Why not just go for it?"

"That's easy for you to say," Casey said as she took two of the warm flour tortillas from the container and put them on her plate. "It's not your seventy-five grand we're talking about."

Tandy chirped a little laugh as she went back to the stove for the skillet of fajita. "It'll probably be more like a hundred or one-twenty-five by the time you get that termite-infested wreck of a building useable again."

Casey rolled her blue eyes. "Don't remind me," she said, shivering at the memory of the web filled attic room. "I thought I was gonna piss myself when Tucker opened that door and flipped on the light in that horrible room upstairs."

Tandy began to laugh uncontrollably. "I wish I'd had my phone out to get a picture of your face, Casey. It was priceless."

"I'm so glad to liven up the meal," Casey said with a little irritation in her voice. She'd always been deathly afraid of spiders and couldn't help her phobia. "Is this prodding me toward parting with my money because you think this will be a good investment for me or an enrichment of your boyfriend and his family?" she asked possibly a little too sharply and regretted her words immediately after they'd come out of her mouth. "I'm sorry, Tandy. I didn't mean that the way it sounded."

Tandy stabbed at a piece of beef on her plate. "I think you meant it just the way it sounded, Casey, and no, I don't give a rat's ass if the Riley clan and their cowboy town get a little richer off you. I think this could be the next step in your business, is all." Tandy wiped a tear from her cheek, and Casey felt horrible for upsetting her friend.

"I know, Tandy, and I'm so sorry." Casey rose and went into the kitchen, where she mixed two strong gin and tonics. "It's just a hell of a lot of money for the franchise fee, fixing up the place, and then buying fabric to make the product," she said, returning to her seat and swallowing a mouthful of the icy cold drink.

"Damn." Tandy took a sip of her drink. "I forgot about the product. That's gonna take not only money but time. When did Tucker say they planned to open this place?"

"I think he said they were shooting for the Fourth of July weekend."

Tandy glanced up at the Tractor Supply calendar on the wall. "That's only two months away. Do you think you can get everything you need done in that amount of time?"

Casey shrugged. "It really depends on what they're

gonna want, but even for a few racks of simple skirts, bodices, and underthings, it would be a lot of late nights." She rolled meat and vegetables into the tortillas and applied a good helping of sour cream to cool what she knew would be spicy. "I imagine they have an idea of what sort of clothing they're going to want their new Miss Millie to have in her shop—likely very prim and proper sorts of things since Desert Home is going to be a family destination the way *The Drifter* was such a family show."

She and Tandy both laughed. "Girl," Tandy said, pointing her finger at Casey, "I want you to make me the most Madamesque piece of garb you can come up with for me to wear when I prance into that damned Dancehall of Charity's."

Casey grinned. "Miss Kitty from Gunsmoke or Jane Seymour from East of Eden?"

"I'm feeling the wicked Jane in East of Eden," Tandy said with a sigh, "but this is a family venue, so maybe someplace in between."

"Got ya," Casey said, "a decidedly wicked Miss Kitty it is."

They finished their dinner and did the dishes, discussing period fashions of the day and what Casey might want to incorporate.

"It sounds to me like you've decided to do this," Tandy said as they sat on the back porch with more glasses of gin, enjoying the cool spring evening.

"I guess I have," Casey said with a deep sigh, "so I better make a trip back to Santa Clarita to clean out my storage unit and my bank account."

Dinner that night at the big Riley table was almost as tense.

Chris joined them late, washing his hands in the kitchen sink before joining his family at the table. "I think Baby is gonna make it," he told his mother with a reassuring smile, "but it's a damned good thing Tandy and her friend got her to me when they did. It was a bad bite by a big diamondback if I gauged right by the size of the fang marks in her leg."

"Oh, my gracious," Rita Riley gasped," that poor little thing."

Morgan Riley took his wife's perfectly manicured hand. "Don't fret over it, honey. Chris is taking good care of Baby, and she'll be jumping those fences again before you know it."

"I know," she said with tears brimming in her cloudy blue eyes, "but we just lost our little Ringo to a snake last fall and now our poor Baby." Tears leaked down her powdered cheeks. "I couldn't bear losing another of my sweet babies."

"Calm down, now, Mother," Morgan said to his wife as he patted her quivering hand.

"I don't even know why we're still messing with these silly little horses anymore," Charity snapped. "We have our hands full with Desert Home, and the pesky horses just get in the way, chasing them every time they jump the fence and nursing them when they get hurt."

"Oh," Rita moaned as she stood and shuffled away from the table toward her bedroom.

"Now, that was totally uncalled for, Charity," Morgan grumbled at his daughter. "You know how much your mother loves those little horses, and you had no call talking to her like that. You need to apologize to her before you go to bed."

"I'm sorry, Dad," Charity said, running her hand through her auburn hair, "but we just don't have the time or money to screw with those damned little horses anymore. It was fine when we were kids and dressing up like cowboys to visit kids in hospitals, but we haven't done that in ages."

"I thought we planned to feature the horses for kids at Desert Home when we open," Chris said. "Has that changed for some reason I'm unaware of?"

"If you're gonna have your damned horses, Chris," Charity said, "you're gonna have to be the one to deal with the damned things, and I still haven't seen a proposal from you about what your plans are for the damned things." She popped the tab on her can of beer. "Are you thinking of saddle rides or carts, and how much do you propose the saddles and carts will cost? I need that information to work into our budget." She glared at her brother with a cocked brow. "And have you even investigated what the insurance liability for horses with kids is going to cost us?"

Chris glanced at his brother for support. "I'll get right on that, Sis," Chris said. "Is there anything else you need from me for pony and cart rides?"

Charity tossed her napkin on the table in frustration. "Just get me what I asked you for, Chris, and I'll take it from there." She turned to her twin. "And do you have anything to offer, Tucker, or were you just amusing yourself with that slut Tandy and her friend today?"

Chris's eyes went wide. "Tandy is not a slut any more than you are, Charity, so shut up about her."

"She spread her legs for the whole damned football team in high school, Chris. Everybody in school knew that," Charity sneered.

"And you spread yours for the whole dammed basketball team, Charity. They used to say you lived up to your name and were very charitable with all your favors."

"Christopher," Morgan Riley snapped at his youngest son, "don't talk about your sister like that at this table, and I never want to hear anything like that out of your mouth in front of your mother."

Chris winked at his brother. "Sure, Dad, whatever you say." He took a long swallow of beer. "So how did it go with that friend of Tandy's?" he asked. "She's not too hard on the eyes. Is she? I think Tandy said she's recently divorced, so she's available."

Tucker cleared his throat and glanced from his father to his sister. "Casey Miller is a seamstress who's been involved in the Medieval re-enactment scene for several years," Tucker said, "and I offered her the franchise on Miss Millie's place to sell and rent costumes to the people visiting Desert Home."

"Did you happen to get samples of her work, asshat?" Charity sneered at her brother.

Tucker took out his phone and passed it around the table with the photos Tandy and Casey had shared. "She's been at it for some time, and I think she has some good ideas about marketing and merchandising for Desert Home."

"Marketing and merchandizing for Desert Home is our department, brother, not some Ren Faire floozy's," Charity snapped at her brother. "Does she actually have the franchise fee and money to bring Miss Millie's up to snuff because you can't take that shit in trade no matter how cute you think her ass is."

Morgan chuckled at his daughter's comment. "Remember, Miss Millie was very chaste on the show, kids. We can't have a floozie in there."

"We're gonna keep things as true to the show as we can, Dad," Charity promised. "I just hope this woman Tucker has come up with knows her stuff when it comes to historical costuming and isn't just blowing smoke up his skirt."

"Tandy says she does," Tucker said, "and that's plenty good enough for me."

Charity rolled her eyes. "And what the hell does that slut know about anything?" she demanded.

"Charity," her father cautioned. "Those pictures looked pretty nice to me," the old man said. "Let's see if she comes up with the money and what her plans might be for Miss Millie's before we make up our minds about her."

"She's thinking it over," Tucker said, "but we have to have the building fumigated pretty quick."

"Why the hell would we need to do that, Tucker? Haven't you been reading the same financial reports as I have?" Charity demanded with her eyes narrowed. "Our coffers are empty, bro, and we still have to pay for all the advertising for the opening. Why do we need a damned exterminator?"

"Because the room upstairs at Miss Millie's is full of spiders," Tucker said with a grin. "I mean, it looks like something out of an old horror flick up there, and I guess she has some serious issues with spiders."

"Well," Charity countered, "franchisees are responsible for the cost of bringing the buildings into a workable condition." She smiled sweetly at her scowling brother. "I'd say spraying for spiders falls into that category, so it comes under her responsibility to pay for the damned exterminator."

Tucker winked at his brother. "Maybe I'll trade her some new shirts for it," he said with a chuckle as he watched the red rise in his sister's face.

"Just make certain the bitch has the money for the franchise fee, the fix-up of the building, and stock before you go making any more promises we can't afford to honor, Tucker."

5

The women rose early the following morning. Tandy received a call from Chris with a replay of the preceding evening's dinner at the Riley home.

"I'm gonna kick that entitled bitch's ass," Casey heard Tandy snarl as she poured two cups of coffee. "I have a good mind to tell Casey to forget this whole damned thing and hang onto her money."

Casey grinned. Now Chris Riley was getting a dose of what Casey had accused her of the night before, though she didn't feel too sorry for him.

"What's up?" Casey asked when Tandy joined her on the porch with her cup of coffee.

"I don't know," she huffed, "but I'm thinking I want you to go full-on East of Eden with that damned outfit, and then I'm gonna strut into that dancehall and go head-to-head with Miss Charity Riley in her sub-standard garb." Tandy swallowed more coffee. "It'll probably be one of her mom's old costumes from *The Drifter* with plastic geegaws and a damned zipper in the back."

Casey laughed. She and Tandy had discussed television costuming many times, and she'd pointed out zippers that did not need to be there had buttons up the front been used properly. She swore her clothes would be done properly, though she hated making buttonholes with a passion.

"So, what did bitch Riley say this time?" Casey asked as she emptied her cup.

"Well, she repeatedly referred to me as a slut," Tandy said, "and basically called you a talentless bitch without the money to buy into their little cowboy paradise."

"Really?" Casey said. "Well, we'll see about that," she said, jetting to her feet. "Let's go."

Tandy followed her to the car, and they took off for Desert Home. "I'll call Tucker and tell him we'll meet him at Miss Millie's," she said with a soft chuckle. "And I'll tell him you're bringing your very full checkbook and to bring the paperwork to sign."

When they arrived at Desert Home, the Terminix van was sitting beside the building. Casey parked beside it, and they got out. Tucker met them with a smile on his face.

"How's the horse doing?" was all Casey could think to say when faced with his bright smile and amazing brown eyes.

"Horse?" he said in momentary confusion. "Oh, Baby?" he said, recovering. "She's gonna be fine. Chris got her through the night, and she's back on her little hooves already."

"That's good," Casey said as they entered the building.

The Terminix man walked in from the front of the building, and the scent of insect spray followed him. "I sprayed the attic for the Daddy Longlegs and did a booster for termites around the foundation," he said as he pulled off a statement from his metal notebook. "I'd recommend another spraying for the spiders in two months or if you see more of them up there."

"Sure thing, man," Tucker said and showed him out. He turned back to Casey. "So, I gather you've made a decision?" he asked with a bright smile that reminded Casey of a used car salesman who was about to hook a whale into buying a used Skylark for twice what it was worth.

"May I see the franchise agreement?" Casey asked as she took a seat at the dusty trestle table in the dining area. "Does this spell out exactly what you want me to stock in the store?"

Tucker shrugged his shoulders. "I think Charity filled in that section," he said and flipped through the stack of papers until he came to the addendum. "Here you go," he said and pointed to a list of garments and accessories.

"So, she wants me to have rental garments available?"

"Just a rack of simple things for those folks who can't afford to make a permanent investment." He nodded toward the mercantile. "Eddie and Wren up at the mercantile will be handling men's things, so you should stay away from those so you don't cross over into one another's business."

Casey nodded. "I understand that completely," she said as she studied the list. "It seems your sister has been doing her research and has a full list of patterns she wants me to use."

"Do you have a problem with that?" he asked.

"Not so long as they are period—"

"And don't have freakin' zippers," Tandy said with a grin.

"Zippers?" Tucker said with a confused look on his handsome face.

"Zippers aren't commonly used until the twentieth

century," Casey explained, "and I refuse to use them in my clothes."

"No zippers," Tandy said with a grin, "when all you need are drawstrings and buttons."

Casey was about to sign the franchise agreement when Charity Riley walked in with a man behind her. Her breath caught in her throat when she recognized the man. "Jacob?" she said.

"Jake is our site contractor," Charity said with a look of confusion on her face. "You'll have to work with him to accomplish the restoration of Miss Millie's. He's very accomplished and does beautiful work."

Tandy straightened her back with the entrance of Charity. "I think I'll wander over to the barn and check in on the little patient," she said and made her way out of the building.

Charity's eyes followed Tandy out the door. "Well, at least we have breathable air in here now." She returned to what she was saying. "You'll be working with Jake exclusively to bring Miss Millie's back to what it was during the run of the show, but I'm certain you'll find his work excellent."

"I'm very familiar with Jacob Miller and his work," Casey said, unable to catch her breath. "I was married to his brother for fifteen years."

"And I'm familiar with how she can still blow through my brother's money like water poured in a colander."

Casey got to her feet. "I'm not spending anybody's money but my own, Jacob Miller."

Jake snorted. "You took Michael for a ton of cash in the divorce, and now you're just gonna throw it away on this silly costuming thing the way you did for years when you were together."

"I'll have you know that I brought in almost two-hundred grand a year with my silly costuming business, which he was very happy to spend," Casey shot back. "I don't suppose he ever mentioned that, did he, Jacob?"

"No, he didn't," Jacob said before storming out of the building.

Charity stared at Casey with her eyes wide. "I suppose if you raked in cash like that at those little fairs," she said in a condescending tone, "then I guess we can use a seamstress like you here in Desert Home."

"Nobody uses me anymore, lady. I'm done with being used by anybody."

Casey glanced at Tucker, who glared at his sister. She could see he was fearful of losing the sale. Casey didn't know how she felt about being seen as nothing more than a payday for these two. "So when do you plan on having the big Grand Opening here?" she finally asked. "I see that you want me to keep a percentage of my stock as rental costuming. Is there a laundry facility here on-site, or will I need to fit one in here so I can launder the rented garb after each use?"

She smiled when she saw the question had caught both of the siblings off guard.

"That will be your responsibility, of course," Charity was quick to offer.

"Of course it will," Casey said with a sigh. "I saw that you had certain patterns you wanted me to use. Will you want to approve the fabric as well?"

Tucker answered that one before Charity had the time to form a thought on the matter. "You're the professional here, Mrs. Miller. I'm certain we can leave the fabric selection in your capable hands."

"Thank you, Mr. Riley," she said, picking up the pen to sign the franchise agreement and write the biggest check she'd ever written in her life. "How do you want this check made out?"

"Desert Home Holdings," Charity said. "And you're certain this check won't bounce on us?"

Casey glanced up at the woman's sneering visage but didn't dignify the question with a response. She tore the check from her checkbook and offered it to Tucker. Charity snatched from his fingers. "I'm going into town," she said, "so I'll run this to the bank before it has a chance to cool off."

"So, welcome to the Desert Home family, Mrs. Miller," Tucker said, offering his work-worn hand.

Casey took it. "Thank you, Mr. Riley, but please call me Casey. I haven't really been Mrs. Miller for some time now."

"So, what's your next move?" Tucker asked.

"First I'm gonna have a look at that room upstairs, and then I think I'll try to do a little cleaning before I drive back to Santa Clarita and pick up my sewing machines and things in storage there."

Tucker grabbed a broom from the corner in the kitchen area. "I batted down some of the webs up there," he said with a nervous grin, "but this might help in case some of those creepy-crawlies are still on their feet."

"Thanks," she said as Tucker followed her up the creaky stairs. "I really dislike spiders."

Tucker chuckled. "I gathered that." He pushed open the door to the small attic room and flipped on the light that consisted of a single dusty bulb hanging from a strand of insulated wire. The carcasses of hundreds of spiders littered the floor, the dressing table, and a three-quarter-size bed and Tucker batted down the remaining webs that clung to the sloped attic ceiling and wallpaper that sagged because its glue had separated away from the walls sometime during the Vietnam War Era. He cleared his throat. "I can't imagine you'd want to sleep up here," he said, clearing dead carcasses from the dingy bed sheet, "but it'll do for storage."

The strong smell of the poison hung in the space and had begun to give Casey a throbbing headache, though it could have been brought on by any number of other things—Charity's hateful words, the encounter with her former brother-in-law, or parting with such a large part of her divorce settlement with Michael. Casey hoped she could keep her contact with Tucker's twin at a minimum. She didn't think she'd ever met a more disagreeable woman in her life.

They return down the stairs, and Casey felt the first surges of real excitement about this venture. This was her place now—her business and her home. It was old and needed work, but it had potential. If Casey put her mind to it, she knew she could make a go of it. She began to see racks of garments in all the colors of the rainbow and shelves filled with purses and hats to go with all of them. She wished she had her computer here already so she could place an initial order for fabrics and patterns. She would need dress forms and hat stands, a mirror, and a dedicated area for a dressing room. Casey thought this was all going to be so wonderful. It had been a very long time since she'd had anything to look forward to, and it felt good.

"What are you thinking about, Mrs. — Casey," Tucker corrected. "You looked lost in thought there."

Casey smiled. "Just putting things together in my mind," she said. "It'll be a lot to do in only six weeks."

"I know it feels rushed," Tucker said, "but Dad and I thought the Fourth would be a good date for the opening since they always did a big episode every year for that with a parade and fireworks."

"I seriously doubt you'll get a permit for fireworks from the state of California with all this dry tinder up here and these old wood buildings."

Tucker smiled. "You're probably right," he said, "but that doesn't mean we can't get everyone out in their Sunday Best and have one hell of an old-fashioned celebration."

His enthusiasm was contagious. "I bet we could invite a bunch of the SASS chapters up from all over the state and over in Arizona, as well as the Steampunks from San Diego and Phoenix."

She was making lists in her head as they walked from the store area into the living space. "You're gonna want to decorate this as close to the period as you can," he told her, "because we will be giving tours to people from time to time."

Casey smiled. "That won't be a problem," she said. "My storage unit is full of stuff that will work in here." She poked her head into the tiny bedroom. "May I bring down that bed from upstairs to use in here?" she asked. "And where am I supposed to park my car? I was thinking I might get one of those prebuilt barn buildings to use as a garage for it if that's acceptable." She stepped out onto the porch. "What about a garden and a chicken coop?" she asked excitedly. "I thought I could build a chicken coop onto the side of the barn building and then plant a nice garden just there."

Tucker stopped her in mid-sentence with a kiss that took her completely by surprise.

"Wow, well, that's certainly one way to shut a girl up," they heard Tandy say from the yard where she stood with

Chris at her side. "You guys have your business all taken care of?"

Chris grinned and winked at his older brother. "All but the monkey business maybe," he said with a chuckle.

Tandy smacked him on the shoulder. "Now you sound like that bitch sister of yours." She glanced sheepishly at Tucker. "Sorry, Tucker."

Tucker waved his hands in front of his chest. "No need to apologize, Tandy, but calling Charity a bitch may be doing a disservice to bitches everywhere." They all laughed as Tucker slipped his arm around Casey's waist. "Why don't the two of you come on in and let the new Miss Millie tell you the plans for her new shop."

"Does this mean you won't be coming back to the house?" Tandy asked with a glance up into Chris's eyes.

"Only to grab my things scattered around your guest room," Casey said as Tandy and Chris went through the open door into the parlor. "This is Home Sweet Home now."

Chris whistled when he saw the condition of the room. "This is gonna need some serious TLC to make it livable."

Casey took Tandy around and showed her where she thought she'd place certain pieces of furniture and her thoughts on the barn shed for her car, the chicken coop, and the garden.

"Wow, you've really been giving this some thought," Chris said, grinning at his brother. "I think this one might be a keeper, Bro."

"My thought the minute I saw her with Baby in the barn," Tucker said with a glance at Casey. "I think the barn idea is awesome, and Mom and Dad will love the chickens and the garden. Maybe we can get some of the other franchisees to do the same, so we have an actual working old west village up here for folks to see and experience."

Two hours later, Casey had the keys to her new life in her purse and was on her way to Santa Clarita to collect her things from storage. If the LA traffic wasn't bad, she'd be there in four hours and would rent a Penske truck in the morning to drive back to Desert Home.

☙ 6 ❧

Clearing out her storage unit went smoothly with the help of the manager, but when she stopped by Michael's to collect things she'd left behind there, she was met with venomous and unwarranted ridicule from her former husband.

Michael met her at the door with his face red. "Jacob phoned me about this hair-brained business you've gotten yourself into over there, Casey."

"I don't want to fight with you, Michael. I just wanted to pick up my photo albums, my washstand and bowl from the guest bedroom, and some patterns I left in the sewing room."

"The photo albums are where they've always been," he said, "but I tossed all that other shit after you moved out. You know I never cared much for all that used junk you surrounded us with." He grabbed her arm when she tried to move into the hallway toward the bedrooms. "Some of it is still in the garage," he said. "Just take it and go. I don't care to see you or your crap in my house again."

When Casey glanced around the room, she could see

that most of the antiques she'd collected over the years were gone from the house and had been replaced by gauche modern pieces. "Where's my mother's antique pie safe, Michael?"

Michael glared at her. "It's in the damned garage, Casey. Just get it and get out of my hair."

Casey didn't ask her former husband for help and backed the Penske up to the garage doors where she finished filling the truck with the oak pie safe, a drop-leaf kitchen table, four ladder-back kitchen chairs with woven cane seats, the antique washstand she'd saved from a garbage pile and refinished along with its matching porcelain bowl and chamber pot, two nineteenth-century club chairs upholstered in green silk, a corner hutch with stained glass doors on the top, and the earthenware pitcher dating back to the seventeenth century her mother had found for her at a farm sale many years ago. She made room for several folk-art paintings and hoped none of them would get damaged in the crowded truck, but she'd be damned if she'd leave them behind for Michael to throw into the monthly rubbish pile or donate to Goodwill just to spite her.

She pulled up at Miss Millie's and let herself in, relieved to find that the bed from the room upstairs had been carried down, reassembled, and dressed with fresh linens and new pillows in the downstairs bedroom. She didn't know who she had to thank for that, but she certainly would find out tomorrow after she'd had a good night's sleep. Spiders and cobwebs never entered her mind as she crawled beneath the crisp new sheets and fell fast asleep.

Thunderous knocking at Miss Millie's door woke her the next morning. Casey crawled out of bed and wrapped herself in a terry robe to answer it.

Charity Riley and Jacob Miller stood outside, and Casey rolled her eyes, wishing she could return to bed. "Well, your check didn't bounce," Charity hissed, "so I suppose we're stuck with you, Mrs. Miller." She tossed some eight-by-ten glossy color photos on the counter of Miss Millie's Dress Shoppe. "Those are the photos you are expected to replicate in this place as per your franchise agreement," Charity said, "and there's a memo there about a meeting you're expected to attend tonight." She strolled around the building and caught sight of the Penske near the front porch. "As per the franchise agreement, that monstrosity must be out of Desert Home by noon or you'll incur a fine, Mrs. Miller."

"I didn't get in from Santa Clarita until one this morning," Casey said through a yawn.

Charity grinned. "Perhaps you should have started unloading it then instead of taking your lazy ass to bed."

Casey felt her fist clenching as Tucker entered the building. "I brought you some coffee, Casey," he said cheerfully as he put the Starbucks Venti cup into her hand. "If you and lover-boy aren't here to help unload the truck, Charity, I'd suggest you get your lazy asses out so we can get to work on this place."

"I'll be back tomorrow, Casey," Jacob said on his way out behind Charity, "and I'll give you a quote on how much of my brother's money it's going to take to get this dump useable again."

Casey's hand went tight around the cup, and Tucker held her arm. "I brought that coffee for you to drink, sweetheart, and not lob at the back of my sister's and her paramour's heads."

"Thank you, Tucker. I really appreciate it." Casey tipped up the cup and let the hot mocha latte fill her mouth. "How did you know mocha was my favorite?" she asked as the smooth, warm drink flowed down her scratchy throat.

"Because it's mine," he said with a grin as he tipped up his cup and swallowed. "What you say we sweep and mop this nasty floor before we start moving your furniture in here?"

Casey glanced down at the dust-covered planks beneath her feet. "Probably a good idea," she said with a sigh. "I'll go get the broom. Do we even have a mop in this place?"

"In the corner over by the cookstove," he said.

The front door opened and Tandy stepped inside dressed in old jeans and a worn t-shirt. "I'm here to help," she said with a broad smile on her tanned face.

"I'm glad to see you came dressed for the part," Casey said. "That truck is loaded, and the Queen Bitch said I had to have it off the property by noon or be in violation of my franchise agreement."

"She said what?" Tucker asked, rolling his eyes.

Tandy fished her phone from her pocket. "Honey," she said in her sweetest voice, "can you come over to Casey's place and help us unload her truck so your sister doesn't hit her with some fine or other ridiculous Charity bullshit?" Tandy was silent for a minute. "Thank you, sweetness. See you in a bit."

Casey watched Tucker roll his eyes. "Sweetness?" he said with a grin after Tandy had replaced her phone. "Really, Tandy?"

"Well, he is," she said, sticking out her tongue like a petulant five-year-old.

Casey swept while Tandy mopped and Tucker wiped down the dusty walls, peeling off bits of old wallpaper as he went.

"I didn't see any stills of this room in the pile Charity

brought over this morning," Casey said. "Do you think she'd let me get away with just painting in here?"

"What do you have in mind?" Tucker asked.

"Well, the bottom part of the wall is beadboard and the top part is board and batten, so, I thought maybe the top half in a very pastel green and the beadboard in bright white with a darker green chair rail between the two."

"Sounds lovely to me, Case," Tandy said, "but you have a great eye for that sort of thing. You always have."

Tucker shrugged his shoulders. "Sounds nice to me," he said. "I've never been a big fan of wallpaper, and it's a bitch to clean up if you decide you want to change it."

"I just don't want to be in violation of my franchise agreement or anything," Casey said with a grin.

Chris arrived a few minutes later, and the unloading of the Penske began. "You loaded this whole truck yourself?" Tucker exclaimed. "Your husband didn't even help?"

"The man at the storage unit helped with the stuff there, but Michael didn't help with anything from the garage, and I about broke my damned back getting my mom's oak pie safe into the truck. Thank God there was a lift."

They put the pie safe on the wall across from the stove. "It'll be fine there," Casey said, "because I seriously doubt I'll be lighting and cooking with a wood stove no matter how period-perfect I want this place to look and function."

"I know a guy in Yucca who converts these old wood cookstoves to work on gas," Tandy said. "I'll give him a call and have him come out and take a look at this one if you want me to."

Casey glanced at Tucker. "I'm thinking gas would be a hell of a lot safer than wood in this old building."

Tucker shrugged. "I don't care so long as I get some of

Tandy's green chili enchiladas out of it and some of your fried chicken, biscuits, and gravy."

"How about me over here?" Chris protested. "I never even knew either one of them could cook."

As the day neared noon, they emptied the final box out of the truck. She tossed the keys to her car to Tandy. "Would you and Chris mind taking the truck down to Penske? The paperwork is in the glove box, and then stopping by Home Depot for a gallon of bright white, a gallon of pale mint green, a gallon of darker mint for the chair rail, and some pans, rollers, and brushes?" She tossed Tandy her debit card and reminded her of the PIN again. "Grab yourselves some lunch too, and anything else you might need or want."

Chris grinned. "I like your friend, Tandy. She's very generous."

Tucker chuckled. "You've just been running errands for your cheapskate sister too long."

"Too true," Chris said with a sigh. "Can I trade Charity in for this one?"

"Nope," Tucker said, "I'm calling dibs on her."

Chris screwed his face. "You want her for your sister? That's just sick, man, even for our family."

Tandy and Casey began to laugh, and Chris joined in, leaving Tucker looking forlorn until he finally joined in as well. "No, I most definitely do not want her as my sister," Tucker said, leaning in to kiss Casey again. "One of Charity is much more than enough for me."

"For you and me too, brother," Chris said as he put his arm around Tandy's waist and led her outside where he hooked up Casey's car to tow to town and left with Tandy in the Penske.

Casey dropped into one of the club chairs and began to shuffle through the stack of still frame photos Charity had left that morning. "Is there any way I can hire another contractor, or am I stuck with using Jacob Miller?" Casey asked. "I'm just not sure I can deal with him and Charity too."

"Unfortunately, Charity hired him and gave him an iron-clad contract for work here in Desert Home," Tucker said with a shrug. "I'm sorry."

"But I can do painting and wallpapering myself if I want to, right? I don't need a contractor's license to do stuff like that."

Tucker nodded. "That's the way I understand it anyway, but let's not bring it up to my sister because, if there's a hole, she'll likely seal it up for that no-good bastard."

Chris and Tandy returned an hour later with bags of Sonic and large cups of Cherry Limeade. Tucker wolfed down his cheeseburger and tots and then excused himself to shower and change for the meeting at the dancehall with all the principals involved in the Desert Home project.

"I guess I'll see you there," he said with a peck on her cheek. "I know Mom and Dad are excited to meet you."

"Oh, wow," Casey said with a shiver, "no pressure there."

Chris smiled. "Mom and Dad are just regular folks," he said as he stood. "I suppose I'd better be heading out too. Charity demands punctuality at these silly things so she can be the center of attention as she rolls out her latest rules and regulations."

Tandy rolled her big blue eyes. "Sorta makes me thankful I'm not involved."

"The hell you're not," Casey said with a wink at Chris as she gathered up scattered Sonic packaging. "You're my official sidekick. All the old cowboy heroes had a sidekick, didn't they?"

"So, does that make me Andy Devine or Festus?" Tandy asked.

"More like Trigger, I think," Chris said as he scooted out the door. "I will see you girls at the dancehall later."

"I think you have a nice one there, Tandy."

Tandy's eyes followed Chris off the porch. "Yah," she said with a sigh. "I never thought I'd be able to replace my Sam, but Chris is doing a fine job of it so far." She grinned and winked at her friend. "He's very happy my houseguest has finally moved out, though."

Casey dropped down into one of the club chairs and surveyed their day's work. They'd replaced the broken settee with the futon from Casey's storage unit, and the small space looked homier than it had originally. Her folk-art paintings were propped against the wall, waiting to be hung, and the ladder-back chairs now stood around the old trestle table in the dining area.

"Some color on the walls is going to brighten this place up, that's for sure," Casey said. "I'd forgotten how much I enjoyed decorating a new space."

The drop-leaf table stood in the bedroom along with the antique washstand, doubling as a dressing table. "Do you think you'll be comfortable here?" Tandy asked her friend. "You really look beat."

Casey stretched and yawned. "It's been a very long day after another very long day and a late night of driving," she said, glancing at the cans of paint stacked along the wall beside the door. "And I get the feeling it's gonna be six weeks of very long days running one after the next until this place is up and running on the Fourth."

"I'm gonna grab a shower," Tandy said. "You have some clean clothes I can borrow to wear to this shindig?"

"Jeans and sweaters are folded in the bottom of the

armoire and blouses hanging on hangers," Casey said. "Take your pick."

Casey showered after Tandy and reveled in the hot water as it eased away the aches in her sore muscles caused by the strenuous work of the past two days. She used a blow dryer on her red hair and dressed in clean jeans and the Desert Home t-shirt Tucker had given her upon signing her franchise agreement. "Best seventy-five-thousand-dollar t-shirt I've ever owned," she joked as she tucked it into her jeans.

"Well, let's get this over with, shall we?" Casey said as they left Miss Millie's for the dancehall where they could hear loud western music piped into the street via speakers on the exterior of the big building. Cars lined the dusty street, and Casey experienced the first nervous pangs in her belly.

Those pangs became full-blown nausea when she and Tandy walked into the busy dancehall to see every table filled with costumed individuals. Charity stood on the stage in one of her mother's old costumes, staring down at them with a satisfied grin on her face. "And here, folks, is our new Miss Millie," Charity said, "in the finest of what I can only assume are futuristic costumes she's thrown together for our amusement."

The room broke into laughter, and Casey never felt her friend's hand on her elbow as she led her back onto the boardwalk and into the street. "Didn't she tell you this was to be a costumed event?" Tandy asked.

Casey shook her head with tears of embarrassment stinging her eyes. "No, she just said it was mandatory for all franchisees and not to be late."

"The bitch set you up to look bad in front of everybody, including the old man and his wife," Tandy snarled. "Do you have anything else we can change into?"

"Oh, yah," Casey said and grabbed Tandy's hand, charging back down Front Street toward Miss Millie's. "They're Steampunk, but they'll do nicely."

Tandy grinned. "No zippers?"

"Not a single one," Casey said as she hurried through the building and threw open a trunk in the bedroom, pulling out folded garments and tossing them onto the bed.

"Damn, this is gonna be fun," Tandy said as she held a white satin corset up to her abdomen. "I don't think I've ever tried to wear one of these things."

7

Tucker saw the humiliation and discomfort on Casey's face before Tandy pulled her out of the room and she shot his sister a withering glance. This had to be her doing.

"What's everyone laughing at?" Rita Riley asked with confusion etched on her made-up face. "Did Charity make a joke?"

Not a joke, Tucker thought, but certainly, a big mistake, if he read Casey Miller the way he thought he had. She was no woman to be trifled with.

"I don't think I'm very impressed with your replacement for Miss Millie, son," Morgan Riley said, "if she couldn't even bother to dress for this dinner in the proper attire."

Tucker glanced up at his gloating sister again. "I'm sure it was simply a misunderstanding, Dad." Tucker stood. "I'll go and see what's going on." He turned to his younger brother. "Wanna come with me to see what's going on with the girls?"

"What the hell just happened, Tucker?" Chris asked when they got to the street.

"Just our dear sister being our dear sister," he said as they marched toward Miss Millie's.

Chris shook his head. "Tandy doesn't take that sorta shit lightly," he said, "and I don't relish being in the middle of a catfight between 'em."

"Casey?" Tucker called out. "You all right, Casey?" He picked up the flier his sister had left for Casey that morning, and his eyes went wide when he saw the line at the bottom. "She's asking for whatever she gets," Tucker said as he handed the flier to Chris with his finger pointing at the line in red ink that read: Dress casual and comfortable. He saw no mention of period costumes.

Chris whistled beneath his breath when the women walked into the shop area. Tandy wore the teal-and-white striped, mutton-sleeved bodice outfit with her blonde hair done up beneath the white bowler hat decorated with peacock and ostrich feathers. Casey stunned in an unusual black taffeta thing Tucker had never seen before over a white flounced skirt and black and white ostrich feathers in her French bonnet. The combination skirt and blouse fit tight, and the neckline cut low. Her corset pushed up Casey's heavy breasts so they could just be seen beneath the lace modesty panel. Tucker felt his manhood begin to stir in his jeans.

"I hope this is more like it," Casey said as she took Tucker's arm.

"I saw the flier my sister left," he said. "I don't know what she thinks she's doing."

"I don't know either," Tandy injected, "but she's screwing with the wrong women." She opened her matching drawstring bag, took out a folded check, and handed it to Tucker. "I've decided I want to play, too, but as a bit player on the sideline."

Tucker screwed up his face in confusion. "What?"

"Just think of me as a wealthy ranch owner from the next valley who happens to be one of Miss Millie's best customers."

"You sure about that?" Chris asked with his eyes wide.

"Absolutely," Tandy said and kissed his cheek. "I can't let Casey have all the fun around here, and I get the feeling things are going to be getting very fun very soon."

They strolled up the wide dusty street arm-in-arm, and when they stepped into the dancehall, it went quiet.

"Well," Charity said from the stage, "it looks as though our seamstress and her floozy friend have finally found proper attire to join us."

Tandy narrowed her bright blue eyes and marched toward the stage. Charity moved away when Tandy stepped up onto the stage.

"It's gonna start gettin' real now, Bro," Chris whispered to Tucker and nodded toward his cowering sister. "You think Mom and Dad have her well-insured?"

"Hello, folks," Tandy said into the free-standing microphone Charity had been using. "My name is Tandy and this," she said, motioning toward Casey, "is my friend Casey Miller—your new Miss Millie here in Desert Home." She clapped, and the people at the tables followed suit. "We're sorry about our earlier entrance," she said with a withering glance across the stage at Charity, "but there was some miscommunication with our invite to this little shindig from management." She motioned for Casey to join her at the microphone. "So, without further ado, I'd like you to welcome Casey, and I'll leave her with the mike to tell you what her plans are for Miss Millie's."

Casey stepped up to the microphone. "Hello, everyone,

and thank you for welcoming me into your fold." There was more clapping, and Casey smiled. "I've spent the last twenty years or so in California doing costuming for Renaissance and Medieval events." She motioned toward Tandy. "And I've played around some with Steampunk, which lands me here in the nineteenth century with the rest of you." There was more clapping. "I will be putting together an assortment of garments and accessories at Miss Millie's for every woman from underpinnings to outerwear for every occasion."

"Casey takes her costuming very seriously and has been a guest lecturer at Grand Canyon University in Phoenix, where one of her friends teaches theatrical costume," Tandy broke in. "The woman knows her stuff when it comes to things like what fabric in what colors would have been proper to wear and when."

Tucker sat listening as a woman at one of the tables stood to address Casey. "Can you tell me about that outfit you're wearing tonight? I've never seen anything like it." Tucker heard murmurings of agreement around him.

Casey brushed her hands over the apron of her garment. "This is what was known as a Polonaise," she explained, "and it originated as a court garment in Poland in the seventeenth century when those cumbersome panniers were popular, and a woman needed a six-foot-wide seat at the dining room table." Women who knew something about historical fashions tittered while the men just looked confused and kept quiet. "This particular pattern was popular in the early 1870s when the bustle period was just beginning to take hold." She turned so everyone could see the bustled tail of her apron. "In the 1880s, the aprons became more streamlined until the advent of the tulip skirt at the beginning of the Edwardian Era." She ran her hand over her white petticoat. "During this period, any coordinating skirt could be worn, changing the look of an outfit very easily. This particular polonaise is made from black taffeta with white silk ribbon sewn onto it and trimmed with white lace, so I chose a lacy petticoat to wear beneath it. It was designed with evening wear in mind."

Tucker had to admit the woman seemed to know her stuff when it came to historical clothing. He glanced at his father and saw the man with his eyes riveted on the stage, listening to every word Casey said.

"And will you be carrying such as that in your shop?" another woman asked.

"I plan to have outfits to suit every woman's needs," Casey said, and Tucker could see she was beginning to feel at ease with questions she'd fielded at many a costuming seminar in the past.

"Will you be offering community discounts to other Desert Home folks?" someone asked. "And will your garments be manufactured by your hand, or are you bringing them in from China?"

"I will be manufacturing all of my garments right here on-site," she said, "though some of my things like bonnets may have the bases imported and then embellished by me in the shop."

"And are you open to barter?" Ed from the mercantile asked. "I have three girls at home, and having someone here in Desert Home to outfit 'em would be real handy though costly, I'd reckon."

Casey smiled. "I'm gonna need to eat," she said with a shrug, "and I'm more than willing to barter grub for garb." Tucker smiled. This woman knew how to handle a crowd. She must have gotten it from her years at those fairs she'd done.

That brought a laugh from those at the tables, and

Tucker joined her on the stage. "We're all happy to have you here, Casey, but Mom and Dad would like to meet you now, so I'll return the microphone to my sister, and we can get on to the rubber chicken and cold mashed potato portion of our evening."

"I hope you're planning to offer less revealing garments at Miss Millie's, Mrs. Miller," Charity said, staring at Casey's mounded breasts beneath the lace inset. "Remember, this is going to be a family venue, not a gathering of sluts like those Renaissance fairs you're used to."

"Charity," Tucker said in a scolding tone.

"My friend mentioned the bustle period in women's fashion," Tandy said, stepping up to the microphone. "She and I have to wear lacy cushions beneath the back of our skirts to accomplish that extra-large ass look, but some women like Charity here manage it with a few extra biscuits at every meal."

The guests laughed, and Tandy left the stage with Casey and Tucker as Charity took back her microphone, scowling at the women leaving the stage.

"And it's on," Chris said to his brother when they got to their table and took their seats.

Tucker grinned. "Well, Sis certainly had that one coming."

"That's a beautiful outfit, dear," Rita said, admiring Casey's dress. "I wish we'd had such beautiful stuff back in our day on the set," she said to her husband. "Grummond was a great costumer, but even he couldn't have come up with something like that."

Morgan smiled at his wife. "I bet our new Miss Millie here would be more than happy to whip something up for you like that to wear to the Grand Opening of Desert Home, sweetheart."

"Oh, but not in black, Morgan," Rita said in protest. "You know black isn't my color."

"What is your favorite color, Mrs. Riley?" Casey asked in a soothing tone, and Tucker knew she recognized his mother's failing wits.

"I've always loved green or red," Rita said with a broad smile. "I know those are Christmas colors, but they're my favorites."

"I have some beautiful green and red taffeta with gold embroidery on it and some lovely gold to make a skirt from," Casey told her.

"Doesn't that sound beautiful, dear?" Morgan said. "Casey will make you one of her beautiful dresses to wear to the Grand Opening, and you will be as beautiful as you always were on this set."

Charity joined them as the plates of grilled chicken, potato salad, and biscuits were served. She stared from Casey sitting beside Tucker to Tandy sitting beside Chris. "Well, the two of you certainly made spectacles of yourselves tonight."

Tucker took the flier he'd found at Casey's and pushed it across the table to his sister. "Before you start in on them," he said sternly, "perhaps you'd care to explain this to all of us."

"I've nothing to explain," she said, pushing the paper away.

Morgan picked up the flier and read it. "I think you have plenty to explain, girl," he said, glaring at his daughter. "This woman is one of your franchisees in this endeavor, and that entitles her to your respect."

Charity snorted. "I expect my franchisees to dress like respectable women," Charity snapped, "but this one traipses in here looking like a damned whore." Then her eyes traveled to Tandy beside her brother. "And what the hell is that slut doing here? This is an investors' meeting, not a date night." She turned to her father. "I want her gone, Daddy. Did you hear how she spoke about me tonight? It was disrespectful and uncalled for."

Tucker reached into his pocket and took out Tandy's check. "Tandy is now a franchise investor," he said and tossed the check to Charity, who stared at it wide-eyed.

"What can she possibly have to offer as a franchisee?"

"I bought in as Miss Millie's friend and best customer," Tandy said with an impish grin.

"Tandy is also an excellent horsewoman and sharpshooter. She will be adding her horses to our stable for parades and such, as well as putting on shooting demos," Chris said, squeezing Tandy's hand. "She's been doing gun safety classes for years at local schools, and I think that's something we could incorporate into our children's program here as well."

"She also has deep ties with the entertainment industry through her late husband, Sam, who was a stuntman," Tucker said, "and those connections could be invaluable to Desert Home in the future."

"That's a great idea, son," Morgan said with a broad smile. "Welcome to Desert Home, Miss Tandy. I look forward to seeing your show."

"Thank you, sir," she said respectfully. "Now, I just need my seamstress to make me up some riding skirts, vests, and blouses."

Casey smiled and turned to Tucker. "You know she'll want one for every day of the week and special ones for holidays."

"I think I'll work up something special for the opening," Tandy said with an impish grin. "Maybe I'll shoot a whiskey glass off the bustled ass of the saloon keeper."

Charity rolled her eyes and glowered at the large

amount spelled out on Tandy's check. Tucker knew his sister would swallow her pride for all those zeros on the little piece of paper. "Great, now I have to deal with Tandy Oakley and her smart mouth too."

Chris winked at his brother. "Oh, this is gonna be good."

After the dinner, the meeting broke up. Tucker watched as Casey was approached by some of the women to ask about dresses. "I think you were a hit tonight, Casey," Tucker said as he walked with her back to Miss Millie's.

He'd been very attentive all evening, and Casey wondered what this was leading to. She'd enjoyed the kisses but didn't know if she wanted to get involved with a man so soon after splitting with Michael. Technically, Tucker was her boss and her landlord. Would she really want to throw all of that into the mix as well?

He glanced down at those lovely breasts again and felt a stirring in his jeans again.

"Thank you for a delightful evening, Miss Millie," he said when they got to her door. "I'm sorry for my sister's horrid prank." He ran a hand over the taffeta fabric on her arm and smiled, "but you handled it like a pro and came out on top, in my opinion. She shouldn't have done that to you, and I'm sure Dad is going to let her know that." He pulled her close and kissed her. The wine with dinner had relaxed him after the long day. Casey leaned into him. Tucker enjoyed the taste of her mouth in his.

"Thank you, Mr. Riley," Casey said when they finally broke apart, "but I think I'd better get to bed now. Jacob said he'd be here early tomorrow to get started, and I have several buckets of paint waiting for me in the parlor."

"I can't wait to see what you do with the room," he said and kissed her softly this time. "Good night." He turned to leave then turned back again for one last look. "I talked to Dad about your idea for the car barn, chicken coop, and garden, and he thinks it's a great idea, so go for it." The woman had him tied in knots. Would she have invited him in if he'd pushed with one more kiss?

"Thanks," she said and watched him walk away back toward the dancehall and his hidden fifth-wheel.

"Damn," Casey muttered to herself as she tried to ignore the excitement between her thighs and unlock the door. She dropped onto the futon sofa and stared at the cans of paint for a few minutes, imagining what the room would look like with a fresh coat of paint. Then she opened her laptop and went to the fabric supplier's website where she placed an order for twenty bolts of cotton fabric for underpinnings, dresses, skirts, and blouses, as well as thread, buttons, and lace. The order wouldn't fill the shop, but it would get her started. She then placed orders for the patterns Charity had suggested along with some of her own.

Casey went to bed that night with visions of a shop filled with gingham, calico, and Tucker Riley. Did she have it in her to get this all thrown together in six weeks?

8

Casey woke early, put on a pot of coffee, and toasted a bagel. She didn't look forward to the meeting with Jacob, and he didn't disappoint.

"I hope you know what you've gotten yourself into here, Casey," was the first thing out of his mouth when he entered the building. "These assholes want me to put these falling down old set locations back into something habitable, and it's near to impossible with the old slip-shod wiring and next to nonexistent plumbing. They were meant as temporary tv sets, not fucking stores and apartments."

"What more do you think needs to be done in here, Jake?" Casey asked as she handed him a cup of black coffee.

"Got any creamer?" he asked as he took the cup.

Casey found a container of dry Coffee-mate and handed it to Jacob along with a spoon. "Well, I guess we're gonna have to start with shoring up the porches and making new stairs with railings that meet code, check the roof for leaks, and probably reshingle it or clad it in metal.

I'd recommend that against fires. And then we'll move inside and attend to the wiring and plumbing. They used aluminum wiring in most of these buildings because it was so much cheaper back then, and they were only used temporarily, so all of that will need to come out and be replaced with copper."

He went through the building and looked at the kitchen sink and bathroom with its toilet and shower. "I don't guess we need to do much with what you have, but I'll check out the hot water heater."

"I'm gonna need to put in a washer and dryer," Casey said. "I was thinking about a stacked unit beside the refrigerator in the kitchen."

"We can do that," he said. When he saw the paint by the front door, Jacob frowned. "You do realize I have the contract for all the revamping of these heaps, don't you?"

"Tucker said I could do some painting in the living area," she said, "but the store is all yours. I'll need clothing racks in several places, and Charity wants the room to resemble the stills she brought me from the show." She opened the front door to let in some light and fresh air.

Jacob rolled his eyes as they returned to the store. "Good luck finding wallpaper that matches what they used back then."

"So, how much is all of this going to cost me, Jacob?" Casey asked, knowing the amount would be high.

"I'll write you up an estimate tonight after I've gotten up on the roof and had a look, but I'd figure on twenty or twenty-five grand of my brother's money going straight into my pocket," he said with an impish grin.

It was then that Charity came waltzing in. "I'll take some of that coffee," she said when she saw the cups in their hands, "if you have cream and sugar."

"Sugar," Casey said, "but only dry creamer."

"Are you two working out what you're going to do with this place?" Charity asked as Casey poured the coffee.

"I was just telling her I'd give her an estimate as soon as I've checked out the roof and looked at the plumbing and wiring," Jacob said in a much more submissive tone than he'd been using with her.

"Uh-huh," she said, sipping her coffee as she walked back into the store, "and what about in here? Any ideas about what you have in mind?"

Casey cleared her throat and took a deep breath. "Well, in the pictures you left, there was a clothing rack on this wall, one over there on that wall, and some stuff on wooden display mannequins around the room. I just ordered a couple of those last night along with my first bolts of fabric to get things started."

Casey saw Jacob whisper something in Charity's ear and nod toward the other end of the building. "You are aware that Jake has the exclusive contract with Desert Home for all renovations, don't you?"

"Tucker said I could put some paint on the walls in the living area," she said, more than a little irritated at the both of them.

"My brother isn't running this part of the operation, Casey," Charity said in a scolding tone. "If you want to do something with the building or the grounds, you need to clear it with me first, and that's all there is to it."

Casey knew she'd already heard about the plans for the barn building, chicken coop, and garden. "Did Tucker tell you he'd okayed a portable barn building for me to use as a garage for my car, and a chicken coop, and garden area?" she asked hesitantly.

Charity's face grew darker. "And don't think you can go over my head to my father with bullshit like this. You can park your silly little clown car in the parking area with everyone else and buy your damned tomatoes and eggs at Lucky's." She slammed her hand on the counter. "Desert Home is MY operation, and you and your tart friend aren't going to come in here and turn things around."

Tucker came through the front door with his father and walked up behind Charity.

"Fine," Casey said with a glance at Tucker, "I've obviously made a big mistake here," she said and took out her phone. "I'll call the bank and stop payment on my check now." She held out her hand. "I'll give Tandy's check back to her, too, if you'll hand it over."

"What in the name of heaven is going on in here?" Tucker demanded with his father looking on with a scowl.

"This conniving bitch thinks she can stop payment on her damned check and get out of her legal and binding franchise agreement," Charity said, glaring at Casey.

"I don't imagine that agreement is binding at all as Tucker here signed it, and he's not in charge of this operation, you are, as you just told me." She turned to Tucker. "As soon as I stop payment on my check, I'll get another truck and get my things out of here. You should also get Tandy's check back from her so I can give it back to her too."

"What in the name of the good lord did you do now, girl?" Morgan Riley demanded of his daughter. "I gave you a part of this project to keep you out of trouble," he said, "but every time I turn around, you're stirring up more."

"The woman is unreasonable, Daddy, and I think we're better off getting rid of her now."

Jacob took that opportunity to scoot toward the door. "I guess you won't be needing me or that estimate, after all, Casey."

"What is she talking about, Charity?" Tucker

demanded. "What exactly did you do to lose us a hundred and fifty grand just like that?"

"I'm sorry, Tucker," Casey said, "but I can't work under these conditions. If you don't really have any say in what goes on here, then I'm not interested in being a part of this—whatever it is."

"Yes," Casey said into the phone. "I need to stop payment on a check."

"Look at this place, Charity," Morgan said to his daughter, "it already looks a thousand times better than it did on the show, and she has some good ideas about improving the grounds to make Desert Home look just that —a home and not just some old studio set."

Morgan turned to Casey. "Please reconsider, Miss Casey," he pled. "I'll put Tucker in charge of your establishment completely, and you won't have to deal with my contentious daughter again."

"Oh, for Christ's sake," Charity said, stomping her foot like a child about to have a tantrum. "I'm going home. I've had my fill of bullshit for the day. It's all yours, Tucker, see if you can deal with the day-to-day headaches around here." She stormed out, slamming the screen door behind her.

"I'm sorry," Casey said into the phone. "I think things have resolved themselves, and I don't need to stop payment on that check after all."

Morgan smiled. "Now, let's go see where you want to put that barn and garden." He put his arm around Casey's waist." Mother and I love the idea of a chicken coop too. We love the idea of seeing Desert Home as an actual home for people and not just a tourist attraction." They walked through the parlor. "A little paint on the walls and some curtains on the windows is gonna do wonders for this place. Do you think you might consider staying during the offseason as well?"

Casey smiled. "I'll have to if I'm gonna have chickens to take care of."

Morgan tightened his grip on her waist. "I knew I liked you, girl, and Mother does too. She's so excited to get a new dress from you for the opening." He released her waist to take the handrail and go down the stairs. "Just tell me how much it's gonna be, and I think I want to surprise her with one in red and one in green as well."

"It would be my pleasure, sir," Casey said and smiled at Tucker.

They spent the next hour going over where Casey wanted to put the barn and garden area, and they were visited by Ed and Wren from the mercantile who thought the idea of a garage that doubled as a barn would be worth the investment. "And a garden and chickens would be something to keep those kids of mine busy while they're out of school."

"How about a goat for milk?" Wren asked. "Two of the girls are allergic to cow's milk, and a goat wouldn't take up too much space."

"I think Chris was talking about a petting zoo for his children's corner now that he and—uh, Tandy have been putting their heads together on it," Tucker said with a glance at Casey that told her Chris's relationship with her friend wasn't quite common knowledge in the Riley house yet.

Casey accompanied Wren to the mercantile and pointed out a nice spot behind the building for a barn and garden for her and her children. They went inside, and Wren treated her to a cold ginger ale and a piece of freshly baked berry pie.

"You and Charity don't get on very well, do you?" Wren asked.

"Does Charity get on well with anyone?" Casey asked with a grin.

"Only with that thief Jacob as far as I can see," Wren said with a huff. "We paid that man an ungodly sum to restore this place," she said, motioning around the mercantile, "and Ed has had to redo a goodly portion of it at an additional cost to us." She shook her dishwater blonde head. "And Charity didn't do a damned thing about it."

"And Tucker or Mr. Riley?" Casey asked. "Couldn't you go to them?"

"Oh, Charity made it real clear that if we went around her in any way, she'd nullify our franchise agreement and toss us out on our asses with nothing but the clothes on our backs, and we couldn't afford that with three kids to think about." Tears began to slide down her pale cheeks. "We sunk everything we had into this thing," she said.

"I see a lot of potential here," Casey said. "I did Renaissance fairs for years and thought it would be great to have a full-time place to live the historic lifestyle in."

Wren smiled. "We've taken the kids to the big Renaissance Fair in San Bernardino," she said, "but those people don't actually live in their booths all the time. Do they?"

"Some wish they could, considering how much those crooks charge 'em for those booths." She grinned. "Believe me, Charity's got nothing on those greedy sharks."

Wren raised her brow. "So, you know a thing or two about this sort of business."

"I was around it for over twenty years," Casey said, "and worked it from a lowly boothy to a site manager for one of the most popular fairs on the circuit."

"So, you would know something about if the Rileys are doing things the right way or not."

"Yes, I think so," Casey said, "but I see so much potential here in Desert Home, and it's doing something I really love with the costuming."

"We put everything we had into this to give the kids a real historical experience." She smiled. "We had all those awesome westerns when we were kids," Wren said, "but all our kids have are ridiculous sitcoms or shows that glorify the gangster lifestyle we don't want them anywhere near."

Casey nodded. "I understand completely."

Casey spent the afternoon purchasing a barn and making arrangements for its delivery to Desert Home. She had to get Tucker to the sales lot to verify the Riley family's approval, and she got a large discount when Tucker guaranteed the salesman several more purchases from Desert Home franchisees in the near future.

Before returning to Desert Home, Casey stopped by Tandy's and told her everything that had happened that morning, including her discussion with Wren.

"That worries me some, Casey. Can't you use another contractor to get this work done?"

Casey shook her head. "According to Tucker, I can't. Charity wrote the asshat an iron-clad contract, giving him all the repair and refurbishing business at Desert Home."

Tandy smiled. "But contractors can be fired if it can be proven they're doing shitty work."

Casey rolled her eyes. "I guess that means me then, huh?"

"Just take lots of pictures of the stuff he does in your place and then take it to a reputable guy to have it checked out," Tandy said with a shrug of her shoulders. "Hey," she added, "I talked to my friend Barry who does those stove conversions, and he said he'd stop by your place in a day or two to check yours out."

"Cool," Casey said, "I'm dying for a skillet of bacon and eggs."

On her way back to Desert Home, she fished in her bag until she found the card Jacob Miller had given her. She called to tell him she needed that estimate after all.

9

Tucker decided to take advantage of Charity's absence and have a look at her books. He couldn't believe his eyes. Desert Home was solvent, but only just. Even with Casey's deposit and the one he'd made with Tandy's investment, they were going to have a difficult time covering the bills for the advertising they'd planned for the opening.

"Damnit, Charity," he cursed, slamming his fist on the desk, "how could you let it get this bad?"

Tucker dialed his dad and then his brother to set up a meeting to discuss what he'd discovered.

"It's pretty bad, Dad," Tucker said into the phone. "I think we all really need to sit down and have a talk about this without Charity here to make her bullshit excuses. "

Tucker jerked his head up when someone tapped on the door. It was Jacob Miller. "What ya need, Jake?" he asked, certain the man was after yet another check for work Tucker couldn't see as completed.

"Just wanted to let you know," Jake said as he dropped into the chair on the other side of the desk, "I'm putting an estimate together for my former sister-in-law. I'm really glad you and your dad were able to line her out and get her back with the program."

Tucker narrowed his eyes. "There's not a program here, Jake. Desert Home is my father's dream for an educational and entertainment venue."

Jacob smiled and winked. "Yah, right. Tell Charity I'll pad this estimate really good for her. I know she and Casey have a real special love-hate thing going on, and I'm sure she'll enjoy taking a shopping trip into LA on the bitch's dime." He hopped up and left the office with Tucker's eyes following after him. What the hell did he mean by that?

What the hell were his sister and this fool doing to the people of Desert Home? These were all good people, and, like Casey, Tucker had recruited most of them himself. He smiled thinking about Casey in that outfit the other night. Why hadn't he pushed just a little harder to get into her bed? He suspected she'd be awesome in bed and hoped to find out soon.

When he looked up from the books again, Casey was standing in front of him. "I didn't mean to interrupt your work," she said with a soft smile. "I just wanted to let you know I called Jacob and let him know about getting that work started after all."

"Yah, he told me a few minutes ago." He motioned toward the chair. "Please sit down."

"I ... uh ..." Casey muttered.

"Is something bothering you?"

Casey took a seat in the chair, wringing her hands. "I don't know if I should even be doing this," she said with her eyes riveted on Tucker, "but I talked with Wren today from the mercantile, and I have some concerns about Jacob and his work."

Tucker furrowed his brow. "What sort of concerns?" Tucker asked.

Casey then launched into everything Wren had told her about Jacob's shoddy work, Charity's threats about nullifying the franchise agreement if they went to Tucker or Morgan, and their fears about the stability of Desert Home. "I just see so much potential here, Tucker, and think we vendors deserve a fair shake."

"I couldn't agree more, Casey," Tucker said, "and so does my dad. This place is the old man's dream. That television show was his life for almost twenty seasons and brought him and Mom together." He rose and began pacing around the room. "I have no idea what my sister and her carpenter have been up to, but I intend to find out."

"Wren said some of the others are upset too," she said. "Maybe you should go around and have a private word with all of them, but keep in mind that Charity has been holding their franchise agreements over their heads. They're all afraid they're going to lose everything— their franchise fee, all the money they've put into the upgrades, and their time. They're scared, Tucker, and some like Wren and Ed are losing faith in Desert Home because of it."

Tucker walked over and took her hand. "Thank you, Casey," he said, pulling her to her feet and closer to his body. "I needed to hear all of this. It just adds credence to what I've already been thinking." He kissed her cheek. "I'll go around now and talk to everyone, beginning with Eddie and Wren. They were my first recruits into Desert Home, and they're special to me. They're the last people I want to lose faith in me."

"I didn't mean to wreck your day, Tucker. I just

thought it was something you and maybe you dad needed to know about."

"Again, thank you, Casey. It was something I needed to know," he said as she turned away. "I need to get back to Miss Millie's; the man is coming this afternoon to look at the cookstove to convert it from woodburning to gas."

Tucker chuckled. "If you plan to stay here during the winter months, then I'd recommend a heating stove because these old buildings weren't meant for habitation and have absolutely no insulation in the walls."

"I'll keep that in mind," she said as she left the office.

"Damnit," Tucker said, kicking the door shut. "Charity, you've likely ruined our chances here at Desert Home with your greedy, conniving boyfriend." He picked up the accounts book and tossed it across the room. "I just hope I can fix it in time for the opening." He dropped his head into his hands. How could this have happened, and what was it going to do to his father when he found out about it?

❧

As Casey was leaving the office, Jacob stood behind the bar and dialed his phone.

"And how goes it in the shambles, my love?" Charity asked when she answered his call.

"Well, your brother has been holed up in your office for most of the day," Jacob said, "and I just watched my lovely ex-sister-in-law leave, after which Tucker kicked the door shut in somewhat of a foul temper, I'd say."

Charity snorted. "Well, I hope he's gotten a good fill of what I go through every day with those whining wretches he fawns over like a bunch of sniveling children. I have no idea why I let myself get talked into the hair-brained idea in the first place."

Jacob chuckled. "For the money, sweetheart, just like the rest of us, though your brother seemed a little startled at the idea."

"The only thing Tucker cares about is making Daddy and his ridiculous dream come true," Charity snarled. "He has no idea about my skimming from the accounts, and I hope to hell you didn't give it away."

"The bitch called to have me give her the estimate. I assume you'd like me to pad it accordingly and take the regular shortcuts with the work," he said with a chuckle.

"You can wire the place so it burns down around the bitch's head as far as I'm concerned and take the rest of that horrid place along with it," Charity said.

"I'll give her the estimate tomorrow and ask for an advance to get the materials needed," Jacob said, "but you know she's going to be trouble for you as long as she has a business in Desert Home and your dear brother's ear."

"You think that's all she has?" Charity sneered.

"I think the bitch has him between her legs in that bed of hers in that little room," he said with a chuckle.

❧

Tucker went through the account book again, marking things in red ink that he wanted to investigate. Then he left the dancehall and made visits to each of his franchisees. Unfortunately, he heard almost the same story from all of them, and it made him sick to his stomach. Charity had a truckload of things to answer for here, and he wished she was still that little girl their father spoiled. It would certainly do her good to have her hide tanned with the flyswatter. Tucker thought to see that would do him a world of good as well.

When he got to Miss Millie's, he found Casey in ragged

jeans and a paint-stained t-shirt. She had applied blue painters' tape to the facings, window and door casings, and chair rail and had a paint roller in her hand. Most of the upper wall was a soft mint green now, and Tucker thought it looked lovely.

"Wow," he said in a soft voice so as not to startle her, "this looks really nice, Casey."

"Thanks," she said with her cheeks flushing. "I wanted to get this painting done before my fabric shows up and I'm tied to my cutting table and sewing machine."

"How did it go with your appointment?" he asked.

Casey smiled. "Great," she said. "My little wood cookstove will be fully changed out to burn propane in a couple of days, and then I can make you that fried chicken I promised you." She eased the paint roller into the pan. "I asked him about a heating solution for this building," she said hesitantly, "and he said he could put in a propane fireplace that would heat the whole building even though it doesn't have much insolation." Casey walked to the center of the outside wall and pointed. "He suggested we put it here and dress it up with faux river rock and a wide mantel to make it look more period." She cleared her throat. "I'm not gonna get any crap from Charity about having an outsider doing the work, am I?"

Tucker didn't want to get into what he'd found in the books or his conversations with the other shopkeepers. It embarrassed him that he'd allowed his sister to get away with so much right under his nose. "No, Charity won't be a problem here. My dad put Miss Millie's under my direct supervision." He gave her a half-smile. "Just come to me if you want to do something here or have any concerns at all."

"I'm glad to hear that, Tucker," Casey said before

giving him a peck on the cheek. "Would you like some coffee or a beer?" she asked.

He looked at his wristwatch. "Actually, I have a meeting with Dad and Chris, but later maybe?"

Casey returned to her paint tray and picked up the roller. "I'll be here," she said with a smile.

Tucker left Miss Millie's, anticipating his return later that evening. She'd invited him back, hadn't she? Casey was so much different from his ex-wife Elvira, who was a calculating bitch, who could turn a sweet summer day into a raging tornado. Everything the woman said had double meanings, and it had jaded Tucker when it came to women. He spent too much time trying to figure out what they were up to, but he didn't see that in Casey. She seemed to be the sort of woman who meant what she said when she said it. Tucker felt more at ease with her than he'd felt with any woman in a very long time.

He saw his dad's pickup parked by the dancehall and felt the fluttering of unease in his gut. This was not going to be fun, but it had to be done. He marched in to find his dad and Chris surrounded by several of the franchisees. Tucker heard Wren venting, and his gut rumbled again. This was not going to be good.

"Miss Wren here," his father said with an angry scowl on his face, "has been telling us some horrible stories, son. What do you know about this?"

"It was all just brought to my attention today, Dad. It seems Charity and her obnoxious man friend have been up to some hijinks at the expense of our friends and neighbors here."

"It's not just the expense," Morgan said, glancing around at the assembled folks, "but she threatened them with losing their franchise if they didn't keep quiet and toe the line."

"Sounds to me like she was just being our sweet tyrant sister to me," Chris said. "She always was a monster when you gave her a little power."

"Well," Morgan said, "she's gone too far this time, and I intend to straighten her out once and for all." His eyes returned to the folks around him. "I'm so very sorry this happened to you all, and Tucker and I will put our heads together to try and work out some fair compensation for all of you." He nodded toward the door. "Now, if y'all don't mind, I need to go into the office with my boys and have a look at what's been going on in there."

Everyone left them in the dancehall, and Morgan strode, scowling, into the office. "Now tell me what in the name of heaven has been going on here, Tucker. I thought I put you in charge of this operation, but it looks like you've let your sister have run of the place and … and I don't know what," the old man said as he dropped into the chair in front of the desk.

"I suppose I have to take the full blame for that," Tucker said with a deep sigh, "but you're the one who dumped her on me, and I didn't know what to do with her until she offered to take care of the books and run the everyday things around the office."

"Then she brought in her contractor boyfriend to do the upgrades on the buildings," Chris said, "and I'm not sure when they decided to have him get payment from the franchisees for the work. I thought we were paying him to do it."

"Well, it is in the franchise agreement that they'll pay for the upgrades," Tucker said. "If someone buys a Burger King or McDonald's franchise, they have to pay for having the building put up to company specs."

"But it sounds to me like the asshole is charging them for work he's not doing or doing incorrectly," Chris said, "and then when people complained, they were told to deal with it themselves and not go to any of us or lose their franchise completely. That's just wrong, Tucker."

"Anybody know where your sister is?" Morgan asked.

"Jacob probably knows," Tucker said, "but she's likely at the spa in Desert Hot Springs. I saw several payouts to them in the books."

Morgan rolled his filmy brown eyes. "Well, when she gets back, I'm taking her card away, and I don't want her near this office again."

"Then what am I supposed to do with her?" Tucker asked.

"Put her to work swinging a hammer with that contractor of hers," Morgan huffed. Tucker laughed at the mental image of his sister swinging a hammer or doing any kind of actual physical labor. "Or get her ass out there in the dancehall to make it ready for the public on the grand opening. She is Miss Charity, after all, and this is Miss Charity's dancehall and saloon."

"That'll go over like a lead balloon," Chris said with a chuckle.

"I don't care how it goes over," Morgan said as he began to grasp at his left chest. "I think I need my pills, Tucker, and then go home to my Rita."

Tucker yanked open the desk drawer where they kept an extra bottle of nitroglycerin pills for Morgan, who suffered from a mild heart condition. He took out one of the pills and put it under his father's tongue.

"Can you drive him back to the ranch, Chris?"

"Sure," Tucker's younger brother said, putting a hand on his eighty-year-old father's shoulder. "How are you doing now, Dad? Has it passed?"

"Yes, yes," Morgan said, shaking off his son's hand.

"Just drive me home so I can see your mother. You know she always calms me down."

Chris and Tucker helped their father into the passenger side of the pickup, and Tucker watched them drive away. He'd not seen his father this angry and upset in years, and it was all Charity's doing. He kicked a rock in the dusty street and watched it ping off the side of the dancehall. Then Tucker went inside and locked the office door. Charity had a key, but Tucker didn't want anyone else wandering in and seeing how bad things really were at Desert Home.

He flipped off all the lights and then began to wander down the street toward Miss Millie's. A cold beer and Casey's company sounded good. When he went in, he smelled fresh paint and found Casey in the bedroom finishing up the upper portion of the last wall of the small room.

"I don't think I've ever seen anybody sling a paint roller so effectively in my life," Tucker said with a chuckle. He pointed to the embossed tin ceiling panels above her head. "Are you going to paint those too?"

Casey stepped back, staring up at the ceiling tiles that had once been white but now were yellowed with age and coated with dust. "I don't know," she said with a grin, "they sorta work the way they are for that shabby-chic look I'm going for."

Tucker went to the old refrigerator and took out two cold Buds. "I think you should paint them white," he said. "It would do wonders to brighten up this little room."

Casey smiled when he handed her the beer. "Just cleaning fifty years of accumulated dust would likely do wonders."

"I've always wondered how so much dust got in here when the building was closed up tight all that time,"

"Take my word for it," Casey said as she dropped her roller into a bucket of water to soak, "dust can find the tiniest space to get in, especially if there's high wind involved."

Tucker nodded. "We do get some wind up here."

"Good thing that shed company anchors them down good," Casey said. "How did your meeting with your dad go?"

"Not good, I'm afraid. Chris took him home with chest pains."

"Oh, my god," she gasped. "I'm so sorry, Tucker. I feel like this is all my fault."

Tucker put his arm around her. "It had nothing to do with you, Casey." He leaned in and kissed her. "It was all on Charity, not you." He kissed her deeper, and she responded to his need, allowing his hands to wander over her body.

His eyes went wide when her hand found his throbbing manhood beneath his jeans and she unbuckled his belt to release it. "Damnit, woman, you drive me crazy," he whispered.

"Let me lock up and turn off the lights then," she said with a grin, "and we'll see if I can't send you straight to the psych ward."

10

Casey woke to the aroma of coffee and rolled to see Tucker's side of the bed empty. Their night together had been wonderful, and Casey had to admit it had been way too long since she'd enjoyed sex so much.

She rolled out of bed and made her way into the bathroom, where she relieved herself and then brushed her teeth and hair before slipping into some jeans and a t-shirt. She wanted to get her painting finished today, but she also wanted to walk over to the stable and check in on Baby.

When she walked into the parlor, she found Tucker shirtless and sitting on the futon with a cup of coffee in his hand. "I hope I didn't wake you," he said.

"Not at all," Casey said as she went to the Mr. Coffee and poured herself a cup. "Thanks for making the coffee. Would you like a bagel? It's usually what I have since I'm without a stove until this one gets changed over."

Tucker grinned. "It was the least I could do after last night. Thank you, Casey, I really needed that, and a bagel would be nice too."

"I have Plain or Everything," she said.

"Whatever you're having," he said, stretching his muscular arms over his head.

Casey popped two Everything bagels into the toaster. Soon the room filled with the aroma of onions. When it popped up, she buttered it and took it over to Tucker. She bent and kissed him. "I needed it too," she whispered, "and it was wonderful. Thank you."

She padded back into the kitchen in her bare feet and returned with her coffee and bagel. She sat beside him and set the food on the old metal trunk she used for storage and a coffee table. "How's your dad this morning. I thought I heard you talking on the phone while I brushed my hair."

"Chris says he's fine," Tucker told her, "but he and Tandy are taking him in to see his GP just to be sure."

"That's good." She bit into her bagel. "Your parents don't have an issue with Chris seeing an older woman?"

Tucker snorted. "They're just glad he's seeing any woman at all. The asshat let them think he was gay for years."

"Oh, that's just mean," Casey said. "No wonder Tandy is so taken with him. Their personalities are so much alike."

"Ain't that the truth," he said with a chuckle. "But Mom and Dad like her. They always have, and I think she's good for him. He hadn't put anything together for his children's section until Tandy got involved." He chuckled. "Now he comes in with a new idea every day."

"What are your plans for promoting your grand opening?" Casey asked hesitantly.

"I had a lot of big plans," he said with a long face, "but I don't know what we're going to do now that it looks as though Charity has bled us dry."

Casey put her arm over his sagging shoulders. "I worked with a guy at one of the Renaissance fairs who was a marketing guru," she told him. "Let me give it some thought and see what I can come up with that won't cost an arm and a leg."

They chatted for a bit more, and then Jacob came strutting in to see them together on the futon. "Well, doesn't this look cozy," he sneered as he handed Casey the estimate.

Casey studied the paper, knowing the numbers were inflated a good forty to fifty percent above what they should be. "What would these numbers be if I went into Home Depot and picked up the material list myself?" She grinned when his mouth fell open, and he couldn't answer.

"You're estimating ten grand in labor. What exactly is your hourly rate, Jacob?"

"Eh, well, quality work comes at a premium cost," he said smugly. His face turned dark when Tucker began to laugh. "What the hell is so funny, Tucker?"

"Your assertion of quality work on your part, Jacob," Tucker said sternly. "I've been hearing rumors of shoddy and incomplete projects here in Desert Home, so I've hired another contractor to shadow you during this project to keep track of everything, including your billable hours every day."

Jacob's mouth fell open again. "You can't do that, asshole. I have an exclusive contract with Desert Home I'm told cannot be broken. You can't hire another contractor to do the work here."

"This contractor won't be doing a damned thing, Mr. Miller," Tucker said with a grin at Casey. "All he'll be doing is watching to make certain you do the work you're billing Casey for and doing it to code so it won't have to be redone in the future."

Jacob's face turned red, and Casey recognized some of Michael's features in his brother. "You can't do that, you son-of-a-bitch. When Charity gets back here from the spa, we'll see about babysitting contractors." He turned to Casey. "I need fifty percent to get things started if you want this shack up to code by your opening."

Casey smiled sweetly. "Give me a materials list for Home Depot, and I'll have everything delivered," she said with the corners of her mouth trying to turn into a broad smile as Jacob's face got redder and redder. "Then, I'll write you a check for fifty percent of your labor estimate."

"Bitch," he screamed and pointed a finger at Casey. "This is your doing, so I seriously doubt you'll be in code compliance by your big grand opening."

"Mr. Miller," Tucker said in a gruff tone. "If you're refusing to do the work here on a Desert Home franchisees property, then you are out of compliance with your contract, and I know that that makes it null and void in any court of law you'd care to take it to." He winked at Casey. "If that is the case, then I suggest you remove your things and yourself from my property immediately so we can get on with our business."

Jacob glared from Casey to Tucker. "I'll have your damned materials list worked up and get it to you by this afternoon," he said reluctantly before storming out through the store and slamming the door behind him.

Tucker wrapped his bare arms around Casey. "Damn, you're good, woman," he said, kissing her on the mouth hard. "I swear you just gave me wood again with the way you handled that asshole."

Casey smiled. "I've known Jacob for a long time, and it's easy to push his buttons if you know how."

He kissed her again. "And you certainly know how."

Tucker's phone rang. Casey turned when she heard him groan. "It's Charity," he said with a furrowed brow. "I guess he called her whining that we'd been picking on him already."

Casey wandered into the bedroom, found her shoes, and put them on. She started to make the bed when she heard Tucker yelling and went back into the parlor.

"I don't have to explain anything, Charity. Just call Dad, and I'm sure he'll explain everything." Tucker disconnected and tucked the phone into his back pocket. "I'd better get over to the ranch before my sister gives my dad a heart attack he doesn't come back from."

"I'm going over to the stable to see Baby," she said, "and then back to the painting. I hope to have it all finished by tonight."

Tucker came out of the bedroom, buttoning his shirt and carrying his boots. "I'll lock it up when I go and turn off the coffee pot."

She kissed his cheek. "I really did enjoy last night," she said. "I hope we can do it again soon."

Tucker watched her leave with a smile on his face. She was about as far from Elvira as a woman could get. How had he gotten so lucky?

Casey walked to the stable with thoughts of marketing swirling around in her head. Her degree had been in marketing in college, but she'd learned the most about it during her years on the fair circuit. She'd seen things done well and things done horribly wrong. She could see a lot of potential here, but she didn't know what Tucker had in mind for the event, where he wanted to advertise, or how. It was something they'd need to discuss in detail soon. She thought getting the other franchise owners involved would also be good. Letty and Bob at the hotel would certainly be open to suggestions, as would Eddie and Wren, but Casey hadn't really met the others to say how they might react to working with her on promotions. The one person she knew would not be receptive was Miss Charity of Miss Charity's Dancehall and Saloon.

When she got to the stable, she was surprised to see Tandy there with Chris. "Hey, guys," Casey said with a wave as she entered the building that smelled of hay and horses. "I came over to check on our Baby. How's she doing?"

"Up and about like nothing ever happened," Chris said in reply, "but if you're gonna play with her, I'm afraid you're gonna have to wait in line. Silver Sue was here before you, and she brought sugar cubes."

Casey glanced at Baby's stall and saw a woman standing at the door, feeding the little horse sugar cubes from the pocket of her faded jeans that seemed to be three sizes too large. She wore a plaid flannel shirt and, over that, a leather vest from decades ago and a Stetson that had seen much better days. Casey had seen the woman wandering around Desert Home but had never given her much thought. Hadn't there been a character on *The Drifter* called Gold Dust Lil? She was a character sketch of the drunken woman Calamity Jane from Deadwood who dressed like a man and swore like a sailor. As Casey recalled, Gold Dust Lil had been a hard rock miner in the show. Was this Silver Sue taking Lil's place in the revamping of Desert Home?

Casey went back to Chris's office space and grinned at Tandy, who came to her side immediately. "I can tell by that shit-eating grin on your face that something happened last night. Spill it."

"I will never know how our parents managed to sleep together in a full-size bed," Casey said, grinning and glancing at Chris, who seemed busy with paperwork at his desk.

"Well, finally," she said and tossed a wadded paper bag at Chris. "They finally did it, sweetie."

Chris twirled his finger in the air. "So that's why he wasn't at his fifth-wheel all night," he said. "So, where is Casanova now?"

Casey cleared her throat. "He went over to the ranch to check on your dad. Charity called, and Tucker told her to call her dad."

"Oh, shit," Chris hissed. "I'd better get over there too before Dad has another damned heart attack and we have to haul his scrawny ass back to the hospital."

"Morgan was really upset with Charity," Tandy explained, "and well, Rita's not quite all there anymore."

"I know," Casey said with a sigh. "Go on and go with him, Tandy. I feel like this mess is all my fault anyhow." She exhaled. "I never should have brought what I heard from Wren to Tucker, who in turn took it to his dad."

"Don't say that," Chris chided. "Tucker and Dad needed to know what's been going on with Charity and her boy toy. They've been bleeding Desert Home dry with their conniving, and they've been treating our people like crap. Dad needs to just kick both their asses completely out."

"But I certainly never wanted to upset your dad the way I did, Chris," Casey said, wringing her hands. "Had I known about his heart condition, I never would have said anything."

"Again," Chris said, "it wasn't you who caused this, Casey. It was Charity and Jacob, and we needed to know about what they've been doing to our folks." He shook his head. "What they've done is reprehensible." He motioned to Tandy to follow him, and they left the stable together.

Casey walked back to the stall where Baby stood, but she didn't see Sue anywhere. She stepped into the stall and was startled to see the woman sitting against the wall of the stall with her head hanging between her knees.

"Are you all right, ma'am?" she asked.

Sue jerked her head up to stare at Casey. "You're the new Miss Millie, huh?"

Casey offered her hand. "I'm Casey actually," she said with a smile. "But yes, I'm the new proprietress of Miss Millie's Dress Shoppe."

Sue smiled. "I'm sure you're a better dressmaker than Henrietta ever was. That woman couldn't sew a straight line and couldn't even sew on a button without stabbing her fingers."

"Henrietta?" Casey said with her brow furrowed.

Sue smiled. "Henrietta Town – she was the actress who played Miss Millie on the show."

"You knew her?" Casey asked in amazement.

"She was my aunt on the show," Sue said.

"You were Patty?" Casey asked as she studied the woman's aging face. Then she saw it. Patty had a tiny scar on her chin, and this woman had the same scar. "Did you know Tucker and Charity when they were babies?"

Sue snorted and took a bottle of gin or vodka from her pocket. "Morgan's mother and my mother are sisters," she said and took a swig from the bottle. She offered it to Casey, who declined as she cuddled with Baby. "I first got the job as Patty when I was nine, and the twins came along when I was twelve, I think." She grinned. "That was the year I won the award for best young actress for the episode in which Patty saved the ponies from the burning barn." She took another swig from the bottle. "And it was just downhill for me after that."

Casey nodded. "I've heard it can be difficult for child stars when their careers don't take off like they or their parents thought they would."

Sue wiped her nose with her sleeve. "It wasn't that," she said, wiping away a tear as well. A year after they were born," she said, "Rita started bringing the twins to work with her."

She leaned her head toward Casey. "Everyone on set said it was because Rita caught ol' Morgan in the sack with the nanny she'd hired and wouldn't leave them at home with anyone after that." Sue chuckled. "I was just a kid, but kids hear things adults don't expect them to hear or understand." Sue tossed the bottle into a garbage can.

"I was so thrilled when Rita asked me to watch the babies while we were on set. I just never imagined how taking care of two infants would get in the way of my work. My storylines dried up and my parts on screen dwindled to Patty carrying out a bundle of laundry or Patty running out the door to visit friends." Sue shrugged. "I love Tucker to death," she said. "He was such a good baby."

"Charity not so much, I gather," Casey said as she petted Baby.

Sue rolled her eyes. "That spoiled brat squalled night and day for a bottle or just attention, and Morgan gave it to her." She spat into the straw. "By the time *The Drifter* was canceled, I'd aged out of the Patty part and gone on my way," she said. "And Morgan tried to put Charity into the roll as another young Patty." Sue grinned. "You can imagine how that turned out."

"So, what did you do after *The Drifter*, Sue?" Casey asked, genuinely interested.

"I went to college during the flower power days and took acting classes at USC with the money Mom and Dad had saved for me from my work on *The Drifter*." She took another bottle from her pocket and screwed off the lid. "I managed a few bit parts here and there," she said, shrugging her shoulders, "but not enough to put a roof over my head, so I went to work for my dad. He had a contracting business." Sue snorted. I gave up the bright lights and makeup brushes for ceiling lights and paintbrushes," she said with a grunt, "and got my general contractors license."

Casey got to her feet. "Speaking of paintbrushes," she said with a glance back toward Miss Millie's, "I've got a bucket of them waiting for me back at the shop."

Sue got to her feet as well, though it wasn't very graceful, and Casey had to lend her a hand. "I could give you a hand," Sue said. "I'd really love to see the old place again."

"Sure," Casey said with a soft smile at the older woman, who could claim the name Silver Sue because of the amount of it in her stringy, unwashed hair, "why not. Have you eaten today, Sue?" Casey told Baby good-bye and closed Chris's office door.

"I hope you're not planning to use that smokey old woodstove," she said with a grin as she stumbled along beside Casey toward Miss Millie's. "Is it still there, or did someone haul it off to the dump already?"

"That stove is a beautiful piece of Americana," Casey said with a smile, "but I'm having it converted to gas so I can use it without having to figure out how to cook with wood."

Sue slapped Casey's back softly. "That sounds like a good idea to me." When they reached Miss Millie's, Sue stared up at the sign above the door. "That sign could use some paint." She smiled at Casey. "I can take that down and repaint it for you. "I think I remember what it looked like."

"I have pictures," Casey said, "but I have a problem with Charity and her contractor who she's given an exclusive contract for the work here in Desert Home."

Sue followed Casey inside. "Ain't no such thing as an iron-clad contract," she said. "If it can be proven the guy isn't doing his work up to code, the guy is in breach and out of a job."

Casey nodded. "I think that's what Tucker had in mind," she said. "He wants to have someone shadow him and keep track of what he's doing or not doing."

Sue grinned. "I could certainly do that," she said. "My contractor's license is up to date in California."

Somebody pounded on the door, and Casey saw Jacob come through with a piece of paper in his hand. "Here's your materials list, bitch," he spat and tossed the paper at Casey's feet.

Sue bent and picked up the paper. She studied the list. "Did you forget the screws and other fasteners you're gonna need to re-roof this building?"

Jacob shrugged. "I figured the guys at Home Depot would let you know you needed fasteners and shit."

"Or you thought that if I only got what's on the list, you'd have an excuse to hold up my building for the opening," Casey said with her eyes narrowed, and she nodded toward Sue. "This is your shadow, Jacob, and I think you just failed test number one."

"Screw you, Casey, and this drunk old hag too," Jacob hissed before he stormed out of the building.

"Well, isn't he a sweetheart," Sue said.

"My former brother-in-law," Casey said, "and Charity's current boyfriend."

Sue nodded. "Well, that explains a lot." She took the list from Casey. "I can take this list down to Home Depot and get it ordered for you."

II

Casey was nervous sending the woman off with her credit card but, for some odd reason, felt she could trust her. When the Home Depot delivery truck showed up, Casey's mind eased some, and when Sue pulled up with bags of Sonic, she smiled and sighed with relief.

"I hope you don't mind that I used your card to pick up some food," Sue said hesitantly.

Casey smiled. "We have to eat, don't we?" They went into the parlor where Sue stared around the area and her eyes filled with tears. "I really never thought I'd see this place again. I like what you've done with it," Sue said. "I'm glad you didn't cover everything up in that horrid wallpaper the set decorators used to cover all the walls in."

"Tucker said I could do whatever I wanted to do with the living area," she told Sue, "but I have to do the shop the way it was in the show." She noted the woman's dirty hands and hair. "Why don't you go in the bathroom and take a nice hot shower before we eat, Sue, I'm sure you'll be more comfortable."

Sue brushed at her jeans. "All I have are these old

things," she said. "My mama would have called it an affront to the body to cover a clean one with dirty clothes."

Casey got up and went into the bedroom. She returned with a cotton gown and robe. "Here ya go," she said.

They shared the burgers and tots from Sonic and drank tasty cherry limeades. "You have a television?" Sue asked.

"Yah," Casey said. "It's upstairs with a lot of other stuff from my storage unit in Santa Clarita, but I left it in the area at the top of the stairs because that little room up there was full of spiders and webs when I first got here, and I had to have the whole place fumigated."

"Damn," Sue said as she popped a tot into her mouth. "I hate spiders." She chewed. "I have CDs of the old shows in my bag of things and thought we could watch them together to get a look at the way they had the place decked out."

"I have a folder filled with stills that Charity gave me," Casey said and sucked Cherry limeade through the straw, "but watching the episodes might give me an even better feel for this place and Desert Home in general."

Sue looked confused, and Casey continued. "I told Tucker I'd work on some promotional plans for the Grand Opening that he might get on the cheap."

The older woman nodded. Casey thought Sue must be about seventy if her math worked out from what Sue had told her in the barn. "Have you talked to some of the other shop owners here?" Sue asked. "Some of them are really riled up about the crap coming down from that office and are all set to form some kind of HOA and hire a lawyer to make certain their voices are being heard."

"Oh, they've been heard alright," Casey said and went on to tell Sue about what Wren had told her and how she'd gone to Tucker with it, who, in turn, had gone to his father."

"Woo doggies," Sue said with a grin. "I'd reckon Miss Charity is in for an ass-whoopin' when she gets home from wherever it is she's run off to lick her wounds." Sue took another bite of her burger, chewed, and then washed it down with some limeade. "Morgan has put his heart and soul into this project," Sue said. "He paid the studio a chunk of money to buy it, and then gave the twins about a hundred grand in seed money to get things going. Bringing Desert Home back to life is Uncle Morgan's dream."

"Why are you here, Sue?" Casey asked with interest.

Sue shrugged her shoulders. "Well, I'm seventy-three years young, and the old knees just ain't what they used to be," she said with a grin. "The last big quake in LA took down my building, and I just couldn't seem to recover." She shrugged again. "My crews went to work for other contractors, and I got me a little drinking problem in case you hadn't noticed."

Sue smiled and patted Casey's hand when she nodded. "I thought you must have, and it warmed my heart when you trusted me to take your credit card to Home Depot and fill that order the jackass brought over here." She ran her hand through her drying silver hair. "Did you mean what you said about hirin' me to shadow that little fool, or were you just pulling his chain to rile him up?"

Casey smiled. She had been pulling Jacob's chain, but Tucker was the one who'd brought up the shadow contractor thing, and Sue was a contractor who could fill the bill.

"I certainly was," she finally said. "I don't know much about contractor's wages," Casey said, "but, for now, how does ten dollars an hour with room and board sound?"

"Room and board where?" Sue asked, glancing around the room Casey had yet to finish painting.

"Here on my futon," Casey said with a nervous grin, "until I can get the little room upstairs fixed up, and I'm certain all those damned spiders are gone."

Sue smiled. "Ten an hour with room and board sounds more than fair to me if all I'm going to be doing is following that little creep around with my nose up his ass."

"Following him around, maybe taking a few pictures of things he's done, and writing up short reports for Tucker about what you've seen him doing, especially if you think he's done something incorrectly that would be a problem in the future."

"I can do that," Sue said and offered her clean hand to Casey. "Looks like you've got yourself a shadow contractor," she said with a grin, "and a roommate."

Casey cleared her throat for the next statement. "No drinking, though, Sue. I can't have you climbing ladders and such after you've finished off one of those bottles you carry in your pocket."

Sue's face darkened. "I understand, Casey, and I've been cuttin' back since I've been up here. Those bottles this morning were more soda water than gin, anyhow. It's almost impossible to be a hardcore drunk on Social Security benefits," she said with a chuckle. "I may be a bit surly for a few days while I'm drying out, but I'll be spending those with the little creep, so that may work out just fine for all of us."

She and Casey both laughed until someone knocked on the door. Casey got up and opened it to see Tucker standing there. "Hi, Tucker," she said, "come on in and join the party."

"Sue?" Tucker said in amazement when he saw his

cousin sitting on Casey's futon. "What are you doing here?"

"Sue is going to be our shadow contractor to watch over Jacob," Casey said, "and part of her compensation package is room and board here with me."

Tucker hugged Sue but came away looking dumbfounded. "Shadow contractor?"

"Remember I took over Daddy's business when he passed," Sue said, "and I've maintained a valid contractor's license in the state for over thirty years."

"Oh, yah," Tucker said, "but how did this all come to be?" he asked as Casey handed him a beer.

"Well," Sue said before Casey could put together her thoughts, "that surly little creep showed up here with his materials list for Casey to take down to Home Depot, and I took one look at it and knew what he was up to."

"What was that?" Tucker asked with a raised brow. "And how could I prove it to fire the bastard."

Sue grinned and winked at Casey. "Well, he ordered metal roofing panels but didn't bother listing screws to fasten them down with or felt to go beneath them. He asked for plumbing pipe to run to the washer but didn't bother asking for fittings or pipe solder to put them together with." She sipped her limeade. "He also didn't have roof deck on there when I know this old building needs new decking because over half the damned shingles are missing and likely have been for years." She turned to Casey. "I added all those things to the order, and it brought the total up a good bit. Hope ya don't mind."

Casey shook her head. "Not if it is going to be needed, I don't."

"And what did you make of all this missing material on his list?" Tucker asked.

"The jackass wanted good reasons to delay the project

so Casey couldn't be ready by the opening," Sue said. "If he had the roof peeled off then didn't have roof deck or screws on site, he could hold up the project for days, waiting for it." Sue shook her head. "He ordered new treads for stairs but no screws or nails to put them together with and the stuff for clothes racks but no dowels to hang the hangers from. The little creep must have spent hours figuring out what not to put on his list."

Tucker shook his head. "Thanks, Cuz, I'm sure glad you were here to catch this before it was a problem. I should take all this to Dad and fire Jacob's ass today so we can get someone else in here to finish everything before the opening."

Tucker turned to Casey. "That's the other reason I stopped by," he said. "I wanted to tell you I'd be staying at the ranch for a few days to keep an eye on Mom and Dad because Charity will be home tonight or tomorrow, and I'm sure there's gonna be hell to pay there."

Casey got up and wrapped her arms around Tucker's neck. "I don't envy you that," she said and kissed him deeply. "If you need anything, you have my number. Just give me a call."

"You have no idea how good that makes me feel, Casey. I haven't had anybody to lean on for a very long time."

Sue snorted. "That Elvira witch wasn't much support to lean on, was she?" she said and sucked the last of her limeade from the cup with a loud gurgling sound.

"No, she wasn't, Cuz," Tucker said with a chuckle.

Sue stood. "I'm gonna go upstairs and start cleaning up my new room," she said. "You have any of that pretty green paint left I can use on the walls?"

"Yes," Casey said, "or we can run down to Home Depot tomorrow and pick up any color you want."

Sue smiled as she grabbed the broom, mop, and bucket from the corner. "The lighter colors will be fine in that small space," Sue said, "but I am gonna need a bed if you don't mind advancing me enough for a twin bed and mattress."

"Mom has some twin beds in the attic at home," Tucker said, "but you'll need a mattress and box springs."

Casey grinned at Sue. "One thing down," she said, "and only about a hundred and ten to go."

Sue left them, and Tucker kissed Casey after he heard Sue go up the stairs. "I haven't seen my cousin look that good in years," he said. "Thank you, Casey."

Casey smiled. "Do you mean clean or sober?"

"Both," he said.

"I think she just needed something to occupy her time with again," Casey said as she collected Sonic wrappers to throw in the trash. "I think being recognized as a contractor again made her feel needed."

Tucker kissed her. "And maybe finding a friend."

"We all need to feel needed and wanted, Tucker. I think Sue lost that when she lost her business, and that's why she turned to gin for comfort."

"You talked to her about drinking on the job, right?"

Casey rolled her eyes. "Of course I did, and I think she'll be fine with it. She said she'd been cutting back since coming up here to Desert Home."

"I don't suppose you've had time to think about any promotional ideas, have you?"

"Maybe a few things," she said, "but I haven't had much time to put anything on paper yet."

"All right," he said. "I better get over to my fifth-wheel and throw a few things together to take with me to the ranch."

"Have you ever considered putting in a few RV spots

here with electricity and water?" she asked. "That might attract multi-day visitors if they had a place to camp for a few days."

Tucker grinned. "I'll go you one better," he said. "What would you say about little cowboy cabins sort of like those old roadside hotels back in the fifties along Route 66?"

"Wow," Casey said. "Where did that come from?"

"I saw an article on the counter at the shed guy's the other day about people around the country turning their sheds into tiny houses, and the photos reminded me of a place we stayed one time when I was a kid and Dad took Chris and me fishing. I thought I could get about ten of those sheds and dress 'em up inside with a little bathroom, beds, and a kitchenette and rent 'em out as part of the Desert Home experience."

"That's an awesome idea, Tucker," Casey said with a broad smile and her mind racing through possibilities. "Could I make a suggestion then?"

"Of course. I'm eager for your input."

"Make a list of people you think could be vitally important to the advancement of Desert Home and send them all invitations to the opening with a weekend in a cowboy cabin to enhance their cowboy experience to the fullest."

Tucker hung his head for a minute and then brought it up with a bright smile on his handsome face. "I can't believe I never thought of that," he said. "A free weekend for the opening costs us nothing and could buy us hundreds of dollars in future business." He hugged Casey tightly. "You're a genius, Casey, and I just might have to hire you as our marketing director at Desert Home if this pans out."

Casey rolled her eyes. "I'll give you what I can, Tucker,

but my fabric order will be here in a few days, and I'm gonna be busy as hell chained to my sewing machine."

Tucker kissed her again. "Maybe Sue will be able to help you with the sewing," he said.

"I really don't think Sue's talents run in that direction," she said with a smile. "I hope things go all right with your dad tonight or tomorrow when Charity gets home."

"Me too," he said with a deep sigh, "me too."

12

Tucker drove back to his fifth-wheel and filled a gym bag with clean clothes, his toothbrush, shaving things, and deodorant as he pondered Casey's idea. He couldn't wait to tell Chris about it and get his ideas on the subject.

After looking at the sturdy sheds, he'd taken Chris to look at them, and his younger brother had mentioned how one of the lofted barn buildings would make a great little house for him beside the stable so he could keep an eye on the stock and equipment. Tucker had smiled, knowing his younger brother really wanted a place to stay and have Tandy over without having to sneak her into their parents' house on the ranch and avoid Charity and her foul mouth. He also knew it bothered Chris to make love to Tandy in the same bed where she'd made love to her late husband, Sam.

Thinking about his sister caused a tightening in his gut. He still couldn't believe she'd done what she'd done. Tucker wasn't looking forward to the explosion the confrontation with her was going to cause between her and their ailing father. Charity knew about his failing heart, but Tucker didn't think his self-centered twin sister gave a damn about anybody but herself and wouldn't hold back if their father removed her from the position she'd given herself at Desert Home and fired Jacob Miller for cause.

Tucker knew their father had already contacted their family attorney, who'd looked over the document Charity had prepared by another attorney. That fact alone hadn't scored her any points, and the attorney had told them to gather written statements from all the franchisees who'd suffered from Jacob's shoddy work. With those statements in hand, they could fire him, and no judge would hold it against them. The man had padded invoices, left work incomplete, and refused to do repairs to the work he'd supposedly done.

When Tucker added the information he'd received from Sue about the man's intent to delay the work on Miss Millie's to keep her from being open for the Grand Opening, Tucker was certain he'd drive into Desert Home and fire the man himself. Ten years ago, Tucker knew the old man would likely have trounced the contractor and sent him packing with bruises and broken bones, but those days were gone. Tucker smiled to himself. Maybe the asswipe would give his father grief, and Tucker could be the one to happily do the trouncing.

As he traveled the dusty ranch roads, Tucker's mind wandered back to his night with Casey and he felt a stiffening in his jeans. It had been ages for him since he'd had a night like that with a woman. Sex with Elvira had always been about her. Once she'd gotten her orgasm, the night would be over even if Tucker hadn't achieved his. Many nights, he'd resorted to finishing manually in the shower while she rolled over and went to sleep.

It certainly hadn't been like that with Casey. She was a

giving lover who'd made him feel wanted and did all she could to make certain he enjoyed his time in bed with her. His manhood grew more substantial as he thought about the things they'd done that he hadn't enjoyed in years. Casey Miller was certainly an amazing woman, and he was glad he'd run into her with Tandy that day in the grocery store.

He was intrigued to hear what she would come up with for cheap promotion for the Grand Opening and wondered what his sister had in mind, if anything, to promote Desert Home. Considering the things he'd discovered in recent days, Tucker suspected she wouldn't have planned anything had she not been receiving a hefty kickback. He shook his head. Their father had dropped this wonderful gift in their laps, and it looked to Tucker as though Charity had done everything in her power to destroy it.

When he arrived at the ranch, his sister's car was parked in the drive along with his brother's. This was not going to be a pleasant dinner. Tucker tensed when he heard dishes crashing and his sister yelling before he reached the door. Maybe there wouldn't be any dinner at all tonight.

He walked in and saw his mother cowering against the door to the study trembling with her confused eyes wide. Charity was yelling, and their father was yelling back when he could get a word in edge-wise. Tucker didn't see Chris as he went to his mother and took her into his arms. "Come on, Mom, you don't need to hear this juvenile caterwauling. Let me take you to your room where it's quieter, and you can watch TV."

"Ok, honey," she said in a trembling voice beside him, "that would be nice."

Tucker walked with her to her room, turned on the

television, and sat his mother in her favorite chair. "I'm sure Dad will be in to check on you in a few minutes, Mom, just sit tight."

"I'll stay right here, Morgan," she said as her eyes moved to the television where the evening news played.

It saddened him to see his mother's mind slipping away so quickly. She now called him Morgan more than Tucker, and that bothered him. Rita had been diagnosed with Alzheimer's the year before, and the disease had progressed rapidly. She was still clear-witted most mornings, but as the day progressed, her mind slipped away. The doctors had suggested a care facility; Morgan refused. He wouldn't see the love of his life in one of those places with a bunch of blithering mindless idiots. He'd keep her at home as long as he could and expected his children to step up and help him with their mother's care.

Tucker heard a heavy dish crash and hurried toward the kitchen where a shattered dish of lasagna slid down the wall beside their father. "What in the name of heaven is going on in here?" Tucker demanded. "I just put Mom in her room. Do you have any idea how frightened that poor soul is, listening to the two of you going at one another in here like a couple of rabid wolves?"

"Oh, lord," Morgan hissed, scowling at his daughter. "I'd better go and see to her," he said and scurried away toward the bedroom.

"Christ, Charity, have you no consideration for the poor woman?" Tucker hissed at his sister. "You know she and Dad are both sick. Are you trying to put both of them in their graves?"

"They'd both be better off dead than here," she spat at her brother, "then we could sell all of this ridiculous old cowboy crap, split the money three ways, and be done with this pitiful life once and for all." She picked up a memorial figurine of Roy Rogers on Trigger and threw it at the wall where it shattered into a thousand pieces.

Tucker grabbed his sister and slapped her hard across the face. "Get out of their house, you vicious bitch, and never come back." He shook his sister and shoved her against the wall. "Oh, and tell your boyfriend he's fired."

Charity twisted her face up into a sneer. "You can't do that, Tucker. Jacob has a contract."

Tucker glared at his twin. "And if you call our attorney, you'll hear from him about all the evidence we have that shows he's broken that contract and can be dismissed." He pointed to the door. "You're both dismissed, Charity, so pack up your things and get the hell out." He yanked the purse off Charity's shoulder and dumped it on the table.

"What are you doing, Tucker?" Charity gasped as tears of rage and frustration rolled down her face, leaving black streaks of mascara through her foundation and blusher.

Tucker grabbed her wallet and found the company credit cards. "Taking back what you no longer have any right to," he said, waving the Visa and American Express cards beneath his sister's nose as he also found the company checkbook.

"Where am I supposed to go, Tucker, if you're taking my cards?" Charity whined.

"I don't know, maybe a hole in the ground with that snake of a boyfriend and use the money you've stolen from the company and the franchisees of Desert Home." He drew back his hand to slap her again but halted himself, knowing that if he hit her again in this state of anger, he wouldn't be able to stop himself and might really hurt her. "Frankly, Charity, I really couldn't care less where you land so long as it isn't anywhere close to me, Mom and Dad, or Desert Home." He pointed to the door again. "Just get your thieving ass out."

Charity scooped up the contents of her bag and hurried off toward her room. He hoped she was packing and would be gone before his parents came back from their room. He found the broom and began sweeping up the broken dishes from the red Saltillo tile floor. Then he scooped up the remains of the lasagna from the wall and tossed it into the garbage can. He was certain their cook and housekeeper Lupe would be in a rage when she saw it tomorrow morning, and Tucker didn't look forward to being the one to explain it to her.

He took his phone from his pocket and dialed Casey's number.

"Hey, Tucker," she said in a cheerful tone. "What's up?"

It was nice to hear her voice, and he smiled. "I just wanted to let you know that we've dismissed both Charity and Jacob," he said.

"Oh," Casey said with a sigh, "then who's gonna put this new roof on that's stacked up outside my building?"

"Would you mind asking Sue if she can recommend somebody who could get on it like yesterday?" Tucker asked.

"She's upstairs painting her room," Casey said. "I'll walk up and take her the phone." Tucker heard a pause and then, "Sue, Tucker's on the phone and needs to talk to you. Just bring the phone back down when you're finished."

"Hey, Tucker," Sue said. He could imagine her smiling. "What can I do ya for?"

"We just fired Jacob Miller," he told her. "Do you think you could round up one of your contractor buddies to come out and take care of Casey's place before the Grand Opening gets here?"

"I'll see what I can do, kiddo, but it's pretty late notice."

"I know, Cuz, but thanks, and whatever you can do will be much appreciated." Tucker disconnected, hoping Sue could find a competent person to finish up Miss Millie's in time for the Opening.

He heard his sister leave her room and slam the door on the way out. He heard her stop in the living room and stepped in to see her taking framed photos and posters off the wall. "You're a terrible thief, Sis," Tucker heard Chris say from his seat in the dark room. "If you planned to steal Dad's memorabilia collection, you should have left your room a little more quietly."

"All this crap is as much mine as yours, little brother," Charity snapped as she took a signed *True Grit* poster from the frame and began to roll it up. "And I'm taking mine before you can take it and give it to your tramp girlfriend."

Chris shot to his feet and lunged at his sister. "I've told you before not to talk about the woman I intend to marry like that."

"Oh, for heaven's sake, Chris," Charity sneered, "you can't be serious. She's ten years older than you and screws everything that comes along."

Chris snorted. "Gee, Sis, I could say the same about you. Now, put Dad's posters down and get the hell out like Tucker told you to."

Charity continued to take posters from the frames. "Bullshit," she snapped. "This crap is mine too, and I'm gonna sell it and get my share now."

Tucker had heard more than enough and grabbed his sister by the back of the neck and yanked her away from the frames and posters, "Nothing is yours until Mom and Dad are both gone and their wills have been read," He said with a snarl as he pushed his flailing sister toward the door, kicking her suitcases along beside her. He opened the front door, shoved his sister out of the house, and kicked her bags out beside her.

"Was that as satisfying as it looked to me?" Chris asked with a grin.

"Absolutely," Tucker replied as he began to replace the posters his sister had removed from the frames. "I just can't believe what a greedy bitch she is."

13

Casey woke to the sound of pounding and scraping above her head and rolled out of bed. She dressed in paint-stained jeans and a ragged REO Speedwagon t-shirt printed when Kevin Cronin still had his long, curly locks that hadn't gone pure white yet. In other words, it was a damned old T-shirt.

As she went to step off the porch, shingles and other debris began to rain down. Casey stepped back beneath the safety of the porch. "What in heaven's name is going on up there?" Casey called to the shadow she saw on the ground below.

"Sorry I woke you, Casey," Sue called down from the roof, "but I thought I'd get these shingles scraped off here before the rest of my crew gets here to take care of this roof job."

Casey heard a vehicle on the dirt road and saw an old Ford pick-up trailing dust headed for the entrance of Desert Home. "Here they are now," Sue said as she climbed down the ladder and onto the porch. She pinched at the bridge of her nose and rubbed her eyes. "First full day without a shot of gin," she said, "and I'm startin' to feel it."

"I'll make some coffee," Casey said. "Are you sure being up on a roof in the hot sun is a good idea in that case?"

"Probably not," Sue admitted as she followed Casey into the parlor that had been fully painted now with bright white beadboard on the bottom half of the walls and dark mint green chair rails and facings. "The rooms look great, by the way. I love that pink trim in the bedroom in place of the darker green. Very girlie."

Casey grinned. "It goes better with the comforter set Tandy gave me for the bed," she said as she filled the pot with water and added fresh coffee into the filter. By the time Sue's crew knocked on the door, the building smelled like fresh coffee, and Casey was taking cups from the cabinet.

Sue introduced Roberto, Alberto, and Manuel Martinez, and then gave them their orders. "This roof needs to be done today," she said. "You'll find everything you need next to the building. I want the roof decking replaced wherever it looks like it needs it, and if there's one leak the next time it rains, I'll be over in Beaumont to take it out of your hides personally."

"Yes, ma'am, Mrs. Carter, Ma'am. You know me and *mis hermanos* do good work, ma'am."

"Well, don't just stand here scratchin' your Mexican asses. Get up there on that roof and get at it. This lady is payin' y'all a five grand bonus to do a quality job in a short amount of time."

"Yes, ma'am," they all said with grins on their faces and disappeared out the front door.

"Damn," Casey said, "I'm glad I'm not the one working for you."

Sue smiled as she filled two cups with coffee and handed one to Casey. "They're good guys," she said, "and needed the work, so I figured I'd offer it to them under my contracting license rather than shopping it around to a bunch of guys who are gonna want to charge you more money." She sipped her coffee. "If they manage to get it finished today and the area cleaned up nice, would you mind writing each of them a seventeen-hundred-dollar check?" Sue asked sheepishly. "It'd be a little over five grand, but just a few dollars, and those guys have families who could really use it."

"Sure, Sue, no problem at all," Casey said. "Thanks for taking it upon yourself to get it accomplished so quickly."

They heard yelling outside and went out onto the porch to find Charity and Jacob yelling up at the roofers. Charity glared up at Casey. "We came to collect Jacob's five grand you promised, Mrs. Miller, and what are these Mexicans doing here?" she demanded.

"They're my crew," Sue said, stepping down off the porch to confront Charity.

Charity used her hand to shield her eyes from the glare of the morning sun. "Sue?" she said in angry surprise. "What's an old drunk like you doing here? Haven't I told you before to haul your fat old ass off Desert Home property? Now go before I call the cops and have you thrown into the drunk tank where you belong."

"Sue is my guest here, Charity," Casey said, "and I think it's you and Jacob who should be going before I call Tucker and tell him you're here harassing his franchisees."

"You owe me five grand, bitch," Jacob snarled, "and I intend to have it, or I'm calling my brother and taking your ass to court."

Sue snorted. "As a licensed contractor, you should know you don't have a leg to stand on, Mr. Miller, as you were found in breach of contract and fired for cause by the management of Desert Home."

"I'm the management of Desert Home, you old drunk, and I want you all off this property now!" Charity screamed, stomping her feet like a child in a tantrum."

"Should we go, Mrs. Carter, ma'am?" Hector called down to Sue from the roof.

"Not if you and your brothers want that five grand at the end of the day," Sue called back. "Just ignore this *chingada* and get back to work."

The three laborers returned to scraping shingles from the old decking. "You two should just go now," Casey said as she took out her phone and dialed Tucker's number. "I hope you're close," she said when he answered, "because Charity is here harassing the guys Sue found to do my roof." She listened for a minute and then said, "Ok, I'll tell her," and hung up the phone.

"Tucker will be here in, like, five minutes and said that if you and Jacob haven't cleared out by the time he gets here, he's having both of you arrested for grand larceny and trespassing on private property," Casey explained.

Charity marched up to Casey and slapped her hard. "You have no right telling me what to do on my property, bitch," she said and slapped Casey again.

With her blood boiling and her face stinging, Casey balled up her fist and punched Charity Riley square in the face. When she didn't go down, she punched her hard in the gut the way her father had taught her as a girl to defend herself against school bullies.

Charity went down hard on her behind with blood streaming from her mouth and nose. She struggled back to her feet and charged at Casey again. Casey sidestepped the woman, turned, and kicked Charity in the behind, sending her face-first into the sand and goat heads growing there.

Charity came up screaming with the sharp, pointed little seed pods stuck in her face and hands. "I'll kill you for this, bitch," Charity yelled with the three roofers laughing maniacally on the roof, Sue laughing in the shade of the porch, and a group of Desert Home residents who'd been drawn by the screaming, clapping for Casey and her victory over the bully Charity.

Jacob was about to punch Casey in the kidney from behind when a horn blared, and Casey turned to see Tucker's pickup run off the road, throwing up sand and gravel behind it as it raced toward Miss Millie's and the people gathered there. Jacob went around Casey and helped Charity to her feet as everyone grew quiet.

"What in the name of heaven is going on here?" Tucker demanded, glaring at his sister. "I thought I told you to get your boy toy last night and get your asses out of Desert Home, Charity, or I'd call the cops and have you both arrested."

"We only stayed last night," Jacob said, "to collect the money Casey owes me."

Tucker rolled his eyes. "Casey doesn't owe you shit, Mr. Miller, and if you and my thieving sister aren't off my property in t-minus five seconds, I'm making that call to the sheriff's office and having you both arrested for fraud, embezzlement, trespass, and assault."

"He wouldn't dare," Charity told Jacob. "He wouldn't want the bad publicity for his precious Desert Home so close to the opening."

"You know what they say in show business, Charity," Casey said with a wink at Tucker. "No publicity is bad publicity, especially if it's free publicity."

Tucker took out his phone and dialed 911. "Yes, this is Tucker Riley out at the old Drifter set west of Yucca, and I have a couple of trespassers here who've assaulted one of my people here." He winked and smiled at Casey and then turned to his sister. "Yes, I can detain them in the jail here, and there are about a dozen witnesses to the assault who will be happy to supply testimony." He clicked off the phone and grabbed Jacob by the arm while Sue grabbed Charity.

"You can't be serious, Tucker," Charity wailed. "You are not taking me to that filthy jail," she screamed as she struggled in Sue's strong grip.

"Oh," Sue said with a loud chuckle, "I've been waiting for something just like this for as long as I can remember."

"Get off me, you fat old drunk," Charity screamed as she struggled to loosen Sue's grip on her arm.

"Just calm down, Charity, and let them have their fun," Jacob said, "and when we get to the sheriff's office, they'll take pictures of your injuries." He chuckled then, "And we'll have my brother sue their asses for assault, bodily injury, refusal to pay agreed-upon compensation, and anything else he can think of, and we'll own this operation before you know it."

Casey walked back to Miss Millie's with Sue and Wren. "I haven't even been able to finish a cup of coffee yet," Casey said with a deep sigh.

"Never a dull moment here in Desert Home," Wren said with a grin.

"I heard some of you have been talking about putting together a merchants' association, Wren," Casey said.

Wren glanced up the street. "Well, that was before we heard Tucker and Mr. Riley had fired Charity and Jacob. Maybe we don't need one now," she said.

"Oh, but I think we do, Wren. We all need to put our heads together about the Grand Opening to do all we can do to assure it's a success for all of us."

"Well," Wren said uneasily, "I think we all want that,

but what can we do? Isn't it the Rileys' responsibility to do the advertising for this thing and get it off the ground?"

"Unfortunately," Casey said, leaning her head in close, "they dumped Charity because she made some unfortunate decisions with the Desert Home money, and now Tucker is struggling with what to do." She opened the door, and they went into Miss Millie's, where Casey made a fresh pot of coffee and popped an Everything bagel into the toaster.

"Oh, Christ," Wren groaned. "We're gonna lose everything we've put into the mercantile," she said with tears filling her eyes. "We've thrown away our children's futures for this ridiculous pipe dream of mine."

Casey wrapped her arms around the younger woman and let her sob. "Listen to me, Wren," Casey said softly. "Your kids are going to be fine, and so are you and Eddie because we're going to put our heads together and make Desert Home work for all of us."

Wren wiped her eyes and blew her nose on a paper towel. "I'll make a few calls and set up a meeting," she said, "but I'll be discreet about the town's financial situation."

Casey squeezed Wren's shoulder. "Thanks, that's probably a good idea, and I'm sorry I dropped that on you the way I did. I—"

Wren stopped Casey mid-sentence. "Don't you dare apologize, Casey Miller," Wren scolded. "It's the first honest information I've heard since we got here, and I'm grateful to ya for letting me know." She blew her nose again and squared her shoulders. "I'll be damned if I'm going to let that hateful thieving woman steal my dream for my kids, though," she said, squeezing Casey's hand. "We'll put together a Merchant's Association and market the hell out of this opening."

Casey smiled warmly at Wren's renewed enthusiasm and hoped she could come up with some ideas to help make it happen. She buttered her oniony bagel, and the women chatted over coffee about their hopes for Desert Home. The coffee pot went dry about the time Casey's stove man arrived, and Wren bid her goodbye, telling her she'd let her know as soon as she'd set up a meeting with the other merchants.

⁂ 14 ⁂

Tucker was surprised and pleased when Casey called and invited him to supper.

"My stove is all lined out, and now I can make you that fried chicken dinner I promised you."

"Tonight?" he asked

Casey chuckled. "Well, my first order of fabric arrived today, and I fear I'm going to be too busy for cooking big suppers for the next few weeks."

"How is it going with the roofing job?" he asked.

"All done," Casey said. "Sue is a real taskmaster. I'm not sure I'd want to be one of her employees."

"Sounds like you've had a fruitful day," Tucker said.

"Do you think you could bring over that bed from your attic you were talking about? We got Sue a mattress and box springs," Casey said with a giggle, "but it's just sitting on the floor up in that attic room waiting for a bed to go on."

Tucker chuckled. "Oh, I see what this is. It's not going to be a romantic dinner for two but a bribe to get Sue a bed."

"Well, if you're not interested in fried chicken, mashed potatoes, gravy, and fresh biscuits," Casey teased, "or seeing my finished paint job in my bedroom, then I suppose we can do it another time."

"Fried chicken and fresh biscuits?" Tucker said with a laugh deep in his chest. "How could I resist an offer like that? What time would you like me there?"

"Well, we only just got back from town and unloaded everything," Casey said with an exhausted sigh, "and I have poor Sue peeling potatoes, so how about in about an hour or an hour-and-a-half?"

Tucker smiled. "I'll see you in an hour-and-a-half," he said. "That'll give me time for a shower and a shave."

"Great, see you then," she said and disconnected.

Tucker smiled all the way back to his fifth-wheel where he showered, shaved, and put on clean jeans and a Desert Home t-shirt. He'd had five-hundred of the shirts screen printed with a likeness of Front Street with Tucker Hughes' jail from *The Drifter* and the date of the opening. He'd given some to all the franchisees and dropped others at stores in Yucca and neighboring communities to give away as a promotion for the event.

He hated the idea of going to his dad for more money to promote the opening, but after taking a hard look at their finances after Charity had gotten her hands into the cookie jar, Tucker thought he might need to.

He'd gone to his dad with Casey's idea about the RV spots and the cabins made from the sheds, and Morgan had loved the idea. They'd gone into Yucca that very day and ordered ten of the buildings, including one for Chris to put up beside the stable and use as his occasional residence.

He made a mental note to speak with Sue about doing the interiors to look like homestead cabins from the 1870s.

If she thought she could get the buildings habitable by the opening, Tucker would need to put his head together with Casey and his dad to see who they thought would be the best people to offer the cabins to for the weekend.

When he arrived at Miss Millie's, his mouth began to water with the aroma of fried chicken in the air. She had the windows open, and the scent greeted Tucker on the porch. Damn, it smells like she's a fine cook too, he thought as he tapped on the door.

Casey greeted him with a soft kiss, wearing a pretty summer dress made from pink fabric that accentuated her skin tone and hair color. Tucker was shocked to see bolts of fabric leaning against one wall and the counter piled with rolls of lace and satin ribbon in a variety of colors.

"Damn," he said, "this looks like work to me."

Casey rolled her eyes. "I only have a month, but I think I can manage it." She grinned and winked at Sue. "I go into production tomorrow," she said, "by chopping up all that cotton in there into five-yard portions then washing, drying, and pressing it all before I begin cutting and sewing."

Tucker screwed up his face in confusion. "Why do all that when it looks like it's already clean and pressed?"

Sue snorted as she set the table with Casey's pretty Bavarian china. "You ever buy a new shirt you really loved and then run it through the washer once and have it come out a size or two smaller than you bought?"

Tucker thought of a Western shirt he'd bought to wear to a rodeo once that had shrunk badly after Elvira had washed it and frowned at the memory of the nasty fight afterward. "Yah," he said, "I did."

"Well, that's because the manufacturer didn't pre-wash the fabric before cutting and sewing it," Sue said with a grin. "Cotton is notorious for shrinkage, and Casey here knows enough to make certain she's not going to end up with unhappy customers because that nice-fitting bodice shrunk too much to fit over her boobs the next time she tried to wear it."

"Some of that may be poly-cotton and won't shrink much," Casey said, "but I'd rather be safe than sorry later on and lose future sales." She turned to Tucker. "I think you'll see that the folks who do these costumed events do more than one every year and want to have full wardrobes." She went to the stove and pulled the pan of biscuits from the oven. "I'm not just looking for that one sale for the weekend event. I want the lady who's going to love it and come back for all the underpinnings, the day dress, work dress, and party gown sometime in the future."

Tucker's mouth fell open. "I never realized that," he said, suddenly more hopeful of a future for Desert Home. "Are you familiar with any of these groups, Casey?"

"Well, I've heard of a few, but I intend to do some more research. We should get advertisements into as many newsletters as we can about the opening," she said. "Most groups send out paper newsletters to their members, but I'd bet you we could get something on most of their internet sites before the big day to invite everyone out."

Tucker pounded his fist on the table so hard it rattled the china. "I'm so pissed at my stupid sister right now," he raged. "That's the sort of thing she was supposed to be doing all this time."

Casey brought the bowls of mashed potatoes, gravy, and green beans to the table and set them before Tucker. "Don't worry about it, baby," she said and kissed the top of his damp head, filling her nose with the manly aroma of his shampoo. "We'll get it worked out."

"Yah, but it should have been worked out months ago and not a few weeks from the big event."

Not to put Sue in an awkward situation, Casey brought them all tall tumblers filled with ice and root beer rather than bottles of Bud. "Let's eat," she said, and the three of them forked crispy pieces of chicken from the platter and filled their plates with the other offerings on the table.

"Casey here says you're a ruthless taskmaster, Sue," Tucker said with a chuckle. "Did you really whip those poor fellows to get that roof finished today?"

Sue grinned. "You should have seen her houndin' after me to do this or do that to get this damned dinner done for you, Tucker," Sue said and laughed. "No, I didn't have to whip the Martinez brothers. They're good workers when they know there's going to be a good payday at the end of the job."

"Speaking of jobs," Tucker said. "I might have a big one for you."

Sue raised her brow. "What sorta job?"

He went on to tell her about the buildings he'd ordered and his homes to have them livable by the opening of Desert Home. "I know it's asking a lot, and I'd understand completely if you say it's beyond your ability, Cuz."

Sue sat, tapping her temple with her index finger as she thought. "I've seen some of those tiny house deals on the DIY Channel," she said. "You have someone lined up for the concrete work?"

"The setup people from the shed company are doing that and doing a spray foam insulation on the underside of the building as well," he said. "I just need them to look like settlers' cabins with bathrooms, heating, and cooling, and some furniture."

Sue nodded. "I'd reckon me and the Martinez boys could plumb, wire, insulate, and do some rustic finishes for about eight to ten grand each," she said.

"I bet you could offer them up online " Casey said,

"and keep them full all summer and during the hunting seasons for elk and bighorns."

"And fishing up on the lake," Sue said with a wink at Casey. "You just need to make up some nice ads and put 'em in the hunting and fishing magazines." She launched into a sample ad. "Bring the whole family, and they can enjoy the history of the Old West at amazing Desert Home while you kill Bambi's mom or snag a trout," Sue said and laughed. "You could maybe even offer group deals for more than one cabin and family."

Tucker felt his mouth falling open in amazement again. Were these two women the answers to his marketing problem? "The buildings are going to start coming in next week," he said. "I took a few he had on the lot already, and the rest will be coming from the factory in two weeks, including the big lofted barn model we ordered for Chris to go up by the stable, but I think he and Tandy will be doing most of the finishing work on that one. How long do you think it will take you to do one?"

Sue shrugged her shoulders. "I'll know better after we've actually done one," she said, "but I'd imagine me and the Martinez boys could probably knock one out in a day or two if you're not expecting anything too complicated."

"You girls are a godsend," Tucker said. "I think you've just given me a whole new income stream for Desert Home's future." He took Casey's hand and squeezed it.

"Well, let's get back to Desert Home's opening," Casey said as she sipped her cold root beer. "I assume you have a beer and a soda distributor who's going to be supplying the restaurant and saloon?"

Tucker nodded. "I know Charity had that put in place, at least."

"Well," Casey said, "then you should offer them both

outside booth spots somewhere in Desert Home along the parade route and require that they put up posters in every store, restaurant, and tavern where they stock their product." She smiled. "Do you have any idea how much free advertising that will generate when people see the posters everywhere they go in the county?"

Tucker's mouth dropped open again. It was genius. "Don't you think having additional outside booths would upset our regular merchants?" Tucker asked, concerned.

"Not if you offer the same to them should they want it," Casey said.

Tucker looked confused again. "Who might want an additional booth outside their established store?" he asked.

"Well, Mrs. Moore is going to be serving buffalo steak dinners in her restaurant, and she only has about twenty tables in there, so she's limited as to how many customers she can have at one time," Casey said. "What if she wanted to put up an outside booth where she was selling flame-grilled buffalo burgers and fries that people could just walk away with, or say, Wren and Eddie wanted to have a booth selling ice cream cones outside the mercantile?" She picked up her glass. "And maybe somebody else would like to put up a booth selling sarsaparilla in old-time liquor bottles the customers could carry away with them."

"And you offer these outside booths to your Desert Home merchants at no charge," Sue said sternly. "Most of them have already invested enough here and should feel like they are finally reaping a reward out of this whole thing."

Tucker smiled as he buttered one last biscuit. He'd forgotten how forceful his older cousin could be when she wanted to get her point across. "Your bed is out in the back of my truck," he said with a grin. "I suppose you want me to haul it up the stairs and set it up for you too."

"If you'd be so kind," Sue said with a sweet smile on her sunburned face. "This old body spent the day roofing this place, and just now, I overtaxed my old brain trying to think of ways to sell this place of yours."

"Give me a minute to let this marvelous meal settle," he said, patting his belly, "and I'll take care of it for you, sweet cousin."

Sue got up and began clearing the table. "It really was a great supper, Casey. Thank you." She smiled at Tucker. "I'm thinkin' this old gal made herself a good deal here with room and board for a little help fixin' the place up."

Casey snorted a laugh. "We haven't even gotten started on the store yet."

"I'm gonna go get that bed now," Tucker said to Sue. Then he whispered in Casey's ear, "Do you have room for me in your bed tonight if I ask nicely?"

Casey kissed him hard. "Just try getting out of here tonight, Mister Riley," she said with an impish grin.

"Well, all righty then," Tucker said with a broad grin on his face as he left the building. How had he gotten so lucky?

15

The organizational meeting of the Desert Home Merchants' Association gathered in the picnic pavilion at the east end of Front Street and very near Miss Millie's.

"Thank you all for coming this afternoon," Wren said. "I know you all have concerns since the shakeup in management here, and I hope we can ease some of your fears in that regard."

Casey sat at a picnic table beside Tandy and Chris, who'd almost not come because he thought the other merchants might see him as part of management and an enemy rather than another concerned merchant,

"You bought a franchise just like all the rest of us," Casey told him, "and you deserve to be a part of this too."

"Did you all get your letters from Tucker about the outside booths?" Wren asked. "I think that's pretty amazing, don't you?"

Mr. Cooper, the blacksmith, stood with a sour expression on his face. "I don't see how letting in a bunch of outside vendors is going to do any of us any good," he snarled.

"Would you care to take this one, Casey?" Wren asked and sat as Casey stood.

"We wanted to bring in the bottling company that sells Pepsi," Casey said, "as well as the beer distributor, and give them outside booths because, by doing that, we can get them to put up posters for our event in every location they stock their product."

"Can't Riley just ask the stores to put posters up?" Cooper snarled. "Isn't that his job?"

"Mr. Riley has already stuffed locations with the event t-shirts," Casey responded to the sour man, "but the soda and beer distributors can require their vendors to post the signs and pay for the printing of the signs as well." She smiled. "The owner of the beer distributorship was a huge fan of *The Drifter* and even had life-size cardboard cutouts of Morgan and Rita in costume from back then done to stand up in every location to advertise Desert Home, and it was all free to us."

Casey heard impressed murmuring in the crowd. "Have any of you seen the weather girl or sports guy from the two Palm Springs stations yet?" she asked.

"They gonna have booths here too?" Cooper snarled half-heartedly now.

"Mr. Cooper, I'd have thought you'd be jumping at the chance for one of those spaces," Casey said, "then you could fill your inside space with the knives you make and the outside booth with your toys and yard art."

The man's eyes went wide. "I never thought about that, young lady."

"No, the folks from the TV stations won't be in booths," Casey said with a broad smile, "but they will be here as the official spokespersons for the event, and each of them will be appearing on the air the week before the event in full Tucker and Charity garb." She smiled at the applause. "I think they'll be making some guest appearances at the company's sister stations in San Bernardino and Riverside as well, and I think that will get us some serious free publicity, don't you?"

Chris stood and cleared his throat. "I love my brother, and he's a pretty smart guy," he said, "but all of these great marketing ideas came directly from Casey here, and not him."

There was more applause, and Casey felt her face turning red. "Tucker is putting in some rental cabins and RV spots over in that east pasture," she said, "and I'd like to talk to you, Mr. Moore, about offering up a couple of your rooms in the hotel to VIP guests for the opening."

"I only have thirteen damned rooms in that hotel," he said in a surly tone. "Why would I give two of them away?"

"Because they'd be offered to people who could bring a lot more business to Desert Home in years to come."

"Oh, yah, like who?" Moore demanded.

"Like big shots in the Steampunk Society and the Single Action Shooters Society. If we can impress just those two groups enough to get them to hold events here," she said enthusiastically, "it would mean hundreds of dollars in all of our pockets over and over again."

"I know folks in the Shooter's Society," Tandy offered. "I can put you and Tucker in touch with them."

"What about Indians?" Mr. Booth from the tobacco store said. "I bet I could get some of my red brothers in full dress here with teepees if you gave them space for camping and dancing."

Casey smiled. "I'll talk to Mr. Riley about it," she said.

"I bet he'd be thrilled. What cowboy show didn't have an a Native American or two?"

By the time the meeting broke up, Casey had names and contact information for some Native groups, a Mountain Man organization, and another Wild West group that did role-playing events.

Two days later, Wren came rushing into Miss Millie's with a broad smile on her face. "I just saw the weather girl on the Palm Springs station in her Charity garb telling everyone it was going to be warm and sunny for the Grand Opening of Desert Home, the revamped movie and television set where *The Drifter* was filmed back in the fifties and sixties." Her face was flushed with excitement as she threw her arms around Casey. "I think this just might work out," she said with tears brimming in her eyes. "I just don't know what I'm going to do for a booth for the ice cream," she said as they stepped outside for some fresh air.

"I've got ya covered there," Casey said. "One of the things I kept from my Fair days was my booth. It's an eighteen by twenty-four-foot canvas pavilion," she said as she took out her phone and pulled up an old photo of her booth set up at an event. "You'll need a sign, but I'm sure you or Livie can handle that."

Wren grinned. "Speaking of signs," she said, grinning and pointing up to the faded one above their heads on Miss Millie's storefront.

Casey rolled her eyes. "Oh, I know, and the old girl is getting a complete paint job next week so she'll look just like she did when they shot *The Drifter*." She hugged Wren. "Time for me to get back at it," she said.

She spent the rest of the day and late into the night ironing white cotton shirting, plain muslin, colorful ginghams, calicos, poplins, and plaids. Tomorrow she would begin cutting and sewing as Sue and her crew put a fresh coat of white paint on the outside of the old building, red shutters to match the roof and a freshly painted sign above the door.

She and Sue had pasted upholstery fabric that looked almost identical to the paper on the walls in the stills she had from Charity. It had been a struggle wrestling and cutting the wide, ungainly fabric to fit along the stairs, but they had managed, and now all the room needed were clothing racks and clothes.

Her storage building had been delivered, and Sue had built a beautiful coop and wire run for the dozen chickens Casey bought from one of Tandy's friends. It took the birds a few days to acquaint themselves with their new abode and begin to lay again. Now, Casey was getting more eggs than she and Sue could eat, and she was carrying a basket every few days across the street to Wren and her family.

It had been late in the season to put out much of a garden, but Sue had rented a tiller and worked up a space she fenced with split rail covered in chicken wire to keep the rabbits out. Casey planted some tomatoes, peppers, and green beans that were doing well and gave the appearance of a working garden if not an actual one.

"I'm not going to have to bother with the chickens for eggs if you're going to keep us supplied," Wren joked one afternoon as Casey measured her for a new dress to wear for the opening. She'd chosen a blue gingham with narrow white lace at the collar and cuffs along with a small white French bonnet decorated with blue and white flowers. Casey was also making each of the girls dresses in the same style from different colors. The girls would all wear satin ribbons in their hair as married women at the time were the only ones who generally wore their hair up beneath bonnets.

Casey had enjoyed educating the women and girls in Desert Home about fashions of the period and looked forward to a shop filled with customers. As the shop came together, they weren't without their upsets and delays caused by Charity and Jacob. One afternoon they received a visit from a county building inspector. He demanded to see Sue's contractor's license and then wanted to see building permits for everything.

Tucker and his father showed up with reams of paperwork, but all it really took was a gruff Sue to lead the man around by his nose and point things out that were all done to code. It ate up two hours of their day, but in the end, Desert Home flew through the inspections with flying colors and received an operating permit on the spot.

"Damn, that was a close one," Tucker said as they sat down to a supper that night of pork chops, fried potatoes, and slaw.

"No, it wasn't," Sue said with a grin. "I showed him all the things he needed to see and none of the things he didn't need to see." She forked up a chop and bit into it. "I've been at this game for a while, Cuz," Sue said with a wink at Tucker. "And I don't think Charity and Jacob made a very good impression on him when they stormed into his office and claimed Desert Home wasn't up to code and had unlicensed contractors doing the work there without the proper permits." Sue grinned. "He said he pegged them as disgruntled former employees and really didn't want to mess with it, but his boss told him he had to inspect to authorize the operating permit before the grand opening anyhow, so he made the trip out."

"Will that bitch never be out of my hair?" he said, glaring off into the dark outside the window.

"I think he was impressed and will be out with his

family," Sue said. "He watched the show as a kid and was a little star-struck with your dad, I think."

When they'd finished eating, and Sue and Casey had finished the dishes, Tucker lit the gas fireplace. Casey snuggled in beside him to stare at the flames coming up around the ceramic logs. "This is so cozy," she said.

When Tucker had seen the finished product after Mr. Haney had set the final bit of faux stone in place and anchored the mantelpiece, Tucker had ordered fireplaces for all his cabins. "I don't know that they'll be needed that much for heat," he'd said, "but the ambiance is perfect and just what the cabins need."

Chris and Tandy had purchased one for their cabin as well, and Casey noted that her friend was more of a resident in Desert Home than almost anyone else. The kids loved to watch her stunt riding, and she'd even taken on Wren's middle daughter Sarah as an apprentice, though Wren wasn't too happy about the shooting part of the act.

One afternoon just before the opening, as she sat sewing buttons onto some dresses, Casey saw her old pavilion going up across the street. When they saw her, the girls called her over. "Come over and be our first customer, Miss Casey."

Happy for an excuse to set aside her work, Casey folded the piece into her basket and stood. She stretched the kinks from her back and walked across Front Street, where Ed was hanging a sign that listed the ice cream flavors offered. "What can I get for you, ma'am," Sarah asked with the sweetest of smiles as Casey studied the sign.

"Come on, lady," the youngest girl, Ellie, said in a tone Casey knew she'd picked up from Sue. "We have other customers waiting here, you know."

"I'll have the banana split sundae in a waffle cone,"

Casey said with a wink at Sarah, who looked horribly embarrassed by her little sister.

"That'll be three-ten, ma'am," Sarah said.

"Come on, lady, pay up," Ellie prompted in Sue's scolding tone. "We're burnin' daylight here."

Casey reached into her apron pocket and pulled out a five that had been change left from her lunch at the cafe. "Keep the change," she said and moved down the counter where the oldest of the sisters, Livie, prepared the sundae. She piled it high with whipped cream and topped it with a cherry before adding a balsa-wood spoon and handing it to Casey. "Thank you, ladies," she said. "This was just what I needed for a break in my day."

Livie and Sarah rushed out into the street to join her. "We're so sorry, Miss Casey, about Ellie."

Casey smiled. "Are you kidding? People will eat that up. Just let her run with it so long as she doesn't start throwing in Sue's bad words."

Sarah laughed. "She's already had her mouth washed out with soap like six times."

Casey popped the cherry into her mouth. "She'll get the point eventually then."

A few days later, a camera crew showed up with the weather girl and did a tour of Desert Home. The girls made them ice cream sundaes in full costume, and Casey made a big sale to the weather girl who was involved with the Steampunk Society down in Palm Springs and wanted new garb for an upcoming gathering in the Gaslight District in San Diego.

"Your stuff is beautiful," she said, "and I'll be sure to send my friends your way, Miss Millie, when they go ape shit over this, and I know they will," she added off-camera.

"What was that all about?" Tucker asked when he walked up as the camera crew was walking away.

"I just made a big sale," she said. "I tried to give her one of the dresses for free, but she refused, so I simply gave her the quantity discount I extend to my Desert Home family."

They went up into the shade of the porch, and Tucker tipped his hat at the wood mannequin she'd dressed and sat in the swing. "You're lookin' good there, Miss Millie. Lost some weight, have you?"

"I have something in here for you, Tucker," Casey said and opened the door to the shop.

He arched a brow and glanced around as if to see if anybody was listening. "Well, I should hope so," he said and kissed her on the mouth."

She wiggled away from him and went to a rack behind the desk where she took down two hangers. One held a red silk taffeta polonaise and the other, a green one with a long gold skirt hanging with it. "These are the things your dad ordered for your mom," she said.

Tucker fingered the intricate gold embroidery on the green and red fabrics. "This is beautiful, Casey. Mom is going to love it." He studied the garments closely. "And it looks like they'll be super easy for her to put on too."

"Have her try them on, and if they need any adjustments, I'll come right over and take care of it," she said.

"She's been a little under the weather since Charity moved out," Tucker said, "but I bet these will cheer her right up."

"Nothing serious, I hope," Casey said.

"I think Charity has been calling the house when Dad's not there and asking her for money again," Tucker snarled. "I guess she and her boy toy missed their court dates, and now there's a bench warrant out for them, and they're hiding out somewhere."

"Probably with Michael in Santa Clarita," Casey said,

"or the family cabin up in the mountains by Angel's Camp."

"I don't really care where she is so long as she stays far away from me and mine," Tucker said as Casey wrapped his mother's garments in tissue paper and put them in a box to carry home. "Did Dad ever pay you for this?"

Casey smiled. "It's all taken care of," she said and kissed him on the mouth.

Tucker took the box from her hands. "You're a good woman, Casey Miller," He said and kissed her hard and deep. "I think I just might be in love with you," he whispered and left the shop before she could reply—his words echoing in her head.

16

Tucker took the box home and handed it to his father. "It's the stuff you ordered from Casey for Mom," he reminded. "It's all really pretty, and I think she'll like it."

It was steak night at the Rileys', and Lupe had set the table with a huge bowl of fresh greens, baked potatoes with all the fixin's, and of course, a platter heaped with medium-rare beef cut thick the way Morgan Riley liked them.

Morgan handed the box to his wife and kissed her cheek. "Something pretty for the prettiest gal I know," he said as he helped Rita open the box.

Rita folded back the tissue paper and ran a hand over the embroidered taffeta. "Oh, my lord," she said, looking up at her husband. "This is all so beautiful. Is there a special occasion I didn't know about?"

"It's for you to wear at the Desert home Grand Opening," Tucker said, "and Casey wants you to try those on in case she needs to do any quick fixes."

Lupe picked up the box. "Come on back to your bedroom, Miss Rita, and I'll help you to try them on. Isn't that garnet color pretty with all the gold thread running through it?" Rita followed the housekeeper to the bedroom.

"Mom seems a bit more clearheaded today," Tucker said, noting she hadn't called him Morgan or ignored his father as though he weren't even there if Tucker was in a room. "Do you think it's the new medicine?"

"I think it's just because Charity isn't here bugging her for money night and day," Chris said as he began to fill his plate.

Morgan nodded his gray head. "I don't want your sister in this house ever again," he said with a frown. "The day she and her young man left, I saw her hit Rita and call her horrible names." Morgan swallowed beer from the long-neck amber glass bottle and sighed. "I just wish I could block her calls somehow. She upsets your mother so."

"I think I can block her cell number and Miller's," Chris said, "but I can't do anything if she calls from another number.

"Isn't this just gorgeous?" Lupe said as she and Rita returned with Rita dripping in vibrant silk and lace. "And it fits her perfectly. Nothing needs to be changed." Lupe fingered the gold lace on the sleeve. "The woman who made these is a real talent."

"Do you think it's pretty, dear?" Rita asked her husband.

Tucker thought his mother looked amazing for a woman of almost eighty, she still had a shapely figure enhanced by the sparkling silk fabric. He was so happy to see her at almost her old self again. She had good and bad spells. This was one of the good ones, and Tucker hoped it would last through the upcoming holiday weekend.

"I think you'd make a burlap feed sack look pretty,

darlin', but yes, Miss Casey did you up proud. You'll be the belle of the ball on Grand Opening night, and all the cowboys are gonna want to dance with you."

Rita laughed." These old feet haven't danced in years," she said with a girlish giggle, "so I think I'll have to save all my dances for you and only you, dear."

"Why don't you go and try the other one on, darlin'," Morgan told his wife with a nod at Lupe, who was the woman's official caretaker now, "and then come back and have some of this wonderful dinner Lupe has made for us?"

Rita returned wearing the green, and Tucker thought it looked more sedate than the red and would be perfect for his mother's appearances during the day at the event. Morgan had been correct, though, and Casey had done a beautiful job on the garments for his mother. He would thank her tonight.

"Wait a minute," Tucker said and snapped a picture of his mother to show to Casey.

Rita gave him a showgirl pose before she and Lupe returned to the bedroom. Lupe hung the new garments in the closet and dressed Rita in her favorite gown and robe before returning to the table for the family supper.

"Tell your friend Miss Casey that she did an amazing job, son, and that we'll give her credits in any of the photos we're in."

Tucker smiled. Sometimes his father was still caught up in his acting days, and he wondered if he too might have a touch of the same disease afflicting his mother. He shook his head. How would he and Chris handle two parents who couldn't come to terms with reality?

Tucker drove to Desert Home and pulled up to Miss Millie's. The building looked great with the new paint as did all of Desert Home. Red, white, and blue buntings decorated all the buildings, and Tucker could feel the festivity in the air. Locals wandered Front Street, still making preparations for tomorrow's opening and the new RV spots were filled along with the cabins Sue and the Martinez brothers had recently completed. Ten teepees stood on the lot across the road from Desert Home closer to the main road back to Yucca, and campfires burned in pits lined with rock.

Tucker could feel the excitement in the air as he looked up to see Casey stepping out of Miss Millie's with Tandy and Sue.

"Hey, Tucker," Tandy called, "you here to check on all of us reprobates?"

He smiled and walked over to join the women. "No," he said with a broad grin, "I just can't seem to stay away."

"Hey," Wren called from across the street, "come on over for an ice cream cone on the house before the girls, and I wrap this puppy up for the night."

"An ice cream sounds good," Tucker said and squeezed Casey's hand in his.

Wren looked tired, and so did the girls. Ellie and Sarah were already asleep on a pallet in the back corner. "What flavor can I get for you tonight?" Livie asked. "I hope it's butter pecan or lemon so I can get those tubs out of the freezer tonight."

"I'll take butter pecan," Casey said.

"Me as well," Tucker added.

Livie grinned. "Then I hope you two want lemon because I'm all out of butter pecan now."

"Lemon it is," Sue said, and Tandy nodded as well.

"So, I gather you ladies have had a busy day today," Tucker said to Wren as she scooped and filled cones.

"I was a bit leery when Casey suggested I open the ice cream booth for those setting up today," she said, "but she was right. It gave the girls a chance to practice working the booth as a team, and we made more money than I would have figured." She smiled and handed everybody their cones. "And here comes a straggler," she said when Chris came walking up to join them. "What can I get you, Chris?" Wren asked. "Then the girls and I are going to bed."

"A vanilla if you've got it," he said.

"Coming up," Wren said and opened the freezer to scoop ice cream into Chris' cone.

They all walked back to Miss Millie's and went to sit on the front porch. Casey and Tucker took the swing, Tandy and Chris the Adirondack chairs Casey had purchased in Yucca, and Sue settled herself on the top step to gaze out across the road at the teepees and campfires.

"I think you should be proud, Tucker, this has really come together nicely," Sue said as she enjoyed her cone.

"No major incidents to speak of?" he asked nobody in particular.

He'd put Chris in charge of making certain the invited merchants and other guests like the Native Americans were in their assigned spaces. He'd managed things without much trouble with the help of Casey, who had years of experience after her time on the fair circuit. "If you mean did I send anyone to the hospital for being a smart ass, then no," he said with a chuckle, "but I came close when that bunch of calvary guys got here and started talking shit about the Indians." He glared at his brother. "Whose bright idea was it to put the cavalry camp right beside the Indians anyhow?"

"Hey," Tucker said with his eyes wide. "We only have

so much space here, and I had to take into consideration how much people were going to have to walk to see everything." He bit into his cone. "I had to put them there or lose parking space," he said, shrugging his shoulders, "and I didn't think we'd want to do that."

They all flinched when they heard shots fired across the road and then the war whoops of Indians. "Sounds like maybe you should have given up the parking spaces," Casey said with a giggle.

"Putting those garage barns up for everyone was a great idea to gain parking space," Sue said and popped the last bite of the waffle cone into her mouth. "I think this old girl is heading to bed," she said. "Silver Sue is in for a big day tomorrow."

"Yah," Chris said with a yawn. "I think Tandy and I are gonna take one final stroll around the site and then head to bed too." He turned to Casey. "Mom really looked good in those things you made for her," he said, "and she really loved them."

Casey smiled. "Thank you. I hope she didn't have any trouble figuring out how to put them on."

"Lupe helped her, and it was good seeing her in more of her right mind for a change too."

"I'm glad," Casey said. "My Granny lost her wits after some cancer treatments on her skull, and it was hard to watch."

"You never told me about that," Tucker said as he squeezed her hand.

"It was all a long time ago," Casey said, "but I know what you're dealing with, and it isn't easy."

"How did it end with your Granny?" Chris asked hesitantly with a glance at his brother.

"We had to put her into a home when she started

getting belligerent and threw something at her caretaker. She started wandering off too and didn't know where she was or who she was to tell people. Keeping her at home just wasn't an option anymore."

Chris nodded and took Tandy's hand. "Let's go, baby, and try and put those rowdy cowboys and Indians to bed before we have a war on our hands here."

"Good night, you guys," Tandy said with a smile, "and good luck on your sales tomorrow."

"Yah," Casey said with a smile, "and don't you fall off that horse of yours or shoot your eye out."

Chris snorted. "No, she'll probably shoot out mine." He kissed Tandy. "I think it's safe for me to go to bed. All the invited guests have checked in to their cabins and the hotel. I'm sure that if any more cowboys and Indians show up, members of their respective camps will show them the ropes."

Tucker and Casey watched them walk off together hand in hand as there was more shooting and laughter from the camps across the road. "I hope that doesn't go on all night," Tucker said.

"I put a ten o'clock quiet time in the rules," Casey said, "and most of those who do events regularly will respect that."

He stared at her in awe once more. "Wow, I never would have thought of that."

Casey grinned. "Well, you've never tried to go to sleep with somebody doing a very out of key rendition of 'Stairway to Heaven' either."

Tucker kissed her hard. "I never could have done this without you, Casey. You were a godsend, and I appreciate you more than you can know."

Casey kissed him this time. "Why don't we go inside,

turn off the lights, and you can show me just how much you appreciate me," she said with a soft giggle.

Tucker stood and pulled Casey to her feet. "That almost sounded like a challenge to my manhood, Miss Millie," he said with a smile.

"Now," Casey said, "this is a family-oriented event, and Miss Millie would never have invited a man into her house after dark and certainly not into her bed, no matter how much she wanted his manhood."

Tucker chuckled. "You know, that's always something I wondered about."

"What's that?" Casey asked as she moved toward the door.

"Were men and women really that much less interested in sex than we are now? Would a man and woman who wanted one another the way you and I want one another not have gone ahead and had a sexual relationship?"

"I think they did, but the times would have forced them to have been much more discreet about it," Casey said. "I think that even being seen sharing a kiss in public would have been considered so disgraceful the woman and man would have been forced to marry so as not to have been ostracized by the proper, church-going folk in town." Casey took a breath. "And a dressmaker at the time couldn't have been seen as indiscreet, or she'd have had no business except for the saloon and brothel girls who wouldn't normally have been seen there."

"Huh," Tucker said, "so the writers of *The Drifter* got it wrong when they had Charity and her saloon girls going to Miss Millie for new dresses?"

"Absolutely wrong," she said in her teacher's voice. "Saloon and brothel women usually had a seamstress amongst them to make their clothing. No reputable seamstress in a town would sew for fallen women, or they'd get no business from the pure and forthright women in town."

Tucker shook his head. "Things sure have changed," he said and kissed her again, "and boy am I glad of it."

She sighed when his hand found her breast and pinched her nipple. "You and me too, baby. You and me too."

17

Casey woke to the aroma of coffee in the quiet of predawn. The scent of wood smoke from the campfires of the night before hung in the air, and she heard only a few voices through her open window.

She rolled out of bed and took a quick hot shower so her hair would dry before the opening ceremonies and slipped into her white cotton camisole and petticoat. She ran her fingers through her hair as she padded barefoot into the kitchen to find Sue and Tucker at the table with cups of coffee.

"I hope the two of you slept well last night," Casey said as she poured herself a cup.

"I did once all the caterwaulin' quieted down," Sue said.

"I thought the groups did a pretty good job of quieting down by ten," Casey said as she took a seat at the table.

Sue winked at Tucker. "I wasn't talkin' about the caterwaulin' goin' on out there," she said. "I was talkin' about the caterwaulin' comin' from your bedroom, Miss Millie.

I'm guessin' you've got no complaints when it comes to what my cousin here is totin' between his thighs."

Casey felt her cheeks flame and smiled when she saw Tucker's were red as well. "No, ma'am," she said as she tested her coffee. "No complaints at all."

"Damn," Tucker breathed and emptied his cup, "I'd better get down to the fifth-wheel and get dressed. I want to make the rounds of every store, booth, and encampment before we start lining up for the parade."

He smiled. "I got a text from Dad this morning saying the folks at the TV stations have really gone all out, and not only were the guy and gal at Palm Springs in costume this morning, but so were the weather and sportspeople at their San Bernardino and Riverside stations, telling everybody to come out to Desert Home for a weekend of old-time cowboy fun and adventure for the family." He smiled broader. "Can you believe that, and it didn't cost us a dime." He kissed Casey. "You're a genius, woman, and I want to shout it from the rooftops."

Tucker raced out the door after rinsing his cup. "I don't think I've ever seen him so happy, Casey," Sue said. "You've been good for him."

Casey shook her head. "I think getting Charity out of here and getting things back on track is what's been good for Tucker," Casey said.

Someone pounded on the door, and Casey got up to answer it. Wren stood outside with a piece of wet pink gingham in her hand. "Would you happen to have another dress in Ellie's size?" she asked desperately. "The little shit dumped her whole mug of chocolate milk in her lap at breakfast."

"Oh, the joys of motherhood," Sue said with a grin as she took the wet dress from Wren. "I'll throw it in the washer with some pre-treat and wash it up in cold water."

Casey went to the rack of children's dresses and pulled out two in Ellie's size, but neither was pink nor gingham. "All I have is this orangy plaid or this blue calico in her size."

Wren's face fell. "I really wanted to have them all in gingham today," she said, "since we're calling the ice cream booth 'The Gingham Kitchen.'"

Casey went back to the rack and found a red gingham that was the next size larger than what she'd made for Ellie. "This one is red and a little bigger," Casey said with an uneasy grin, "but it's gingham."

Wren took the dress. "And I dare say red suits her temperament much better than pink." She looked at the price tag and took bills from the roll in her pocket. When Casey tried to refuse the money, Wren dropped it on the counter anyhow. "I can't take this out of her hide," the girl's mother said, "but I'm certainly taking it out of her allowance." She turned and left the shop after handing Casey the wooden hanger.

"Well, I guess we'd better get dressed," Casey said. "Sometimes, I made my best sales to the fair participants before the event ever opened," she said with a sigh, suddenly missing her fair days.

Casey dressed in a polonaise she'd created from some of the silk buntings they'd purchased to decorate Desert Home. The bodice and side aprons were red and white stripes trimmed with bunches of wide and narrow white crocheted lace, while the long, bustled tail in the back was blue spangled with bright white stars and trimmed in lace. She wore the polonaise over a full red skirt and topped the patriotic ensemble with a French bonnet sporting red, white, and blue curled ostrich plumes. On her feet, she wore her white lace-up boots.

"Damn, if you don't look like a walking ad for this

shindig," Sue said when Casey came out of her room, pinning the bonnet onto her damp head.

Casey ran her hand over the red poplin skirt and straightened the lace on the apron fronts to even both sides of the polonaise. "You don't think it's too much, do you?" Casey asked nervously.

Sue snorted. "You're supposed to be a creative dressmaker here," she said, smiling at Casey's garb, "and that's about as creative as I've ever seen." She went to the sink and filled two corked bottles with water. "I don't drink anymore," she said, "but Silver Sue does, so I need to get filled up here."

Casey was proud that Sue had clung to her sobriety and thought having the work in Desert Home had accounted for that and hoped she wouldn't fall back into her old ways once Desert Home was on its feet and didn't need a contractor any longer.

Casey hadn't forgotten Tucker's words the day before, but he hadn't repeated them during their lovemaking that night. She hadn't said them to him either and wondered if he was waiting for her to say it. She shook her head as she dressed and arranged dress forms on the porch outside the door to attract clients. She had three inside dressed in party dresses and a full set of underpinnings. Those outside wore simple work and day dresses made from the gingham and calicos.

"You open, Miss Millie?" someone called, and Casey glanced up to see Mandy Jewel, the weather girl from Palm Springs dressed in one of Rita's old Charity costumes along with her full crew of sound and camera people.

"I'm here," she called back, "so I'm open." Casey waved, and they all came hurrying up the steps.

Mandy stepped back to admire Casey's outfit. "Oh my, don't you just look perfect for the day," Mandy exclaimed.

"Bobby," she said to her cameraman. "Get a shot of this lady and me together."

She motioned, and the sound boom made its way over their heads. Mandy was asking questions. "Tell me about this piece of garb you're wearing, Miss Millie." She turned Casey around so the camera could see the bustled piece behind her. "This looks very intricate. Did you make it?"

"I did," Casey said, not bothering to correct her name. She was officially Miss Millie for the weekend now, "and this piece is called a polonaise. A popular garment during the bustle period of the 1870s and 80s."

"Then perfect for our weekend in Desert Home," she said with a bright smile.

They talked a little about the other dresses on the porch, then Mandy cut. "I have three guys here who need at least some shirts and hats for the day," she said, tugging at her gown. "I sure wish they'd let me get something from you," she said with a sigh. "This thing is like a hundred years old, smells like it was never washed, and is heavy as hell."

"Yah," Casey commiserated, "they made that stage costuming heavy."

"And we're not even under any lights," she said as she sipped from a water bottle. "What can you do for my boys here?"

"I'm afraid I don't stock menswear," Casey said, "but Wren across the street at the mercantile has a nice selection of goods for the cowboy, gambler, or gold miner to rent by the day or purchase to take home and use again."

"Oh, good," she said, "I wanted to get another shot of that little imp in the ice cream booth anyhow."

Casey smiled. "Ellie is quite the little rascal, isn't she?"

Mandy smiled. "Reminded me of myself at that age."

Casey watched Mandy and her crew make their way

across Front Street and into the mercantile, then went back to sorting and arranging in the shop. After she heard her hens cackling, Casey went out with a basket to collect eggs from the henhouse. She didn't make it back inside before Mandy and her crew, now attired in western wear, caught her.

Ellie held Mandy's hand and wore her new dress proudly though she had to have it tucked up into her belt to keep from tripping over the hems. "This here is Miss Casey …uh," Ellie corrected herself, "I mean Miss Millie's chicken coop and her garden."

"Ellie tells me you all actually live here in Desert Home, and it's not just your businesses," Mandy said somewhat in awe.

"The concept of Desert Home," Casey said on the spot, trying to think of what Tucker and Morgan might want her to say about Desert Home, "is to put forth an actual Living History situation to show people as much as possible how our forefathers and mothers lived carving out this great nation we have now." She cleared her throat. "Therefore, I have my chickens and my poor little garden that got an unfortunate late start this year."

"And might we get a look into your living quarters? Is that set up in period as well?" she asked.

"For the most part," Casey said, thankful she'd made her bed and done the dishes that morning. "I have electricity," she said with a chuckle, "because there just aren't icehouses anymore to accommodate an icebox." They stepped inside, and Casey flipped on the lights. "I have electric lights rather than oil and a modern toilet. Most of those are for health codes, though I'm happy not to have to squat over a chamber pot in the mornings."

"It's painted up so pretty," Mandy said with a sigh, "and I love all your antiques."

Casey smiled. "I've been a collector for years," she said, "just like my mom who found that old pie safe over there with about a hundred coats of paint on it and took it back down to the honey oak with love and care."

"Oh my God," Mandy gasped, "look at this stove."

"That was an original wood cookstove," Casey told her, "that Ray Haney in Yucca converted to gas for me because the heat from a wood stove in here would be unbearable in the summer for a cup of coffee in the morning."

Mandy made her way to the old Singer machine Casey had found at an antique store recently. "Don't tell me you use this to make the beautiful clothes you sell?" Mandy said.

"I used it to make this," Casey said, running a hand over her red skirt, "but I have an electric machine for the clothes out there on the racks in the shop."

"This is just amazing, Miss Millie," Mandy said as she ushered her crew toward the door. "You've really made history come to life for us today here in Desert Home—your real Desert Home."

"Thanks for visiting, Miss Mandy, and come back any time," Casey said before Mandy and her crew were completely out the door.

"That was great … Casey, I guess it is … that'll make a great supplemental segment on tonight's broadcast. Thanks."

Casey smiled and offered her hand. "It's Casey Miller," she said, "and your guys don't look out of place at all now," she said with a smile. Mandy took her hand. "Thanks, they're really jazzed up about the roleplaying thing, and I'm taking Bobby down to the Gaslight District with me next weekend."

"Have fun, but I'd have put him in gambler digs rather than cowboy for that."

Mandy smiled and shrugged. "You gotta let 'em make their own mistakes."

"Ain't that the truth," Casey said as she watched the young woman and her crew head back to Front Street to check out the rest of the merchants.

Tucker jogged over from the cavalry camp as Casey was about to step back inside. "What was that all about?" he asked, nodding toward Mandy and her crew.

"I was just giving the viewing public a taste of our living history here in Desert Home," she said. "Mandy said she might use it as one of her filler segments this weekend."

"That's fantastic, Casey," he said, glancing around enthusiastically. "Can you believe this? The cars are already lined up to get in. Do you think I should tell them at the gate to start letting them in?"

"I don't see why not, but make certain you tell your people there to let them know the parade won't happen until ten."

"Got ya," he said with a nod before getting on the radio to the people at the front gate.

They stood together on the front porch of Miss Millie's watching the cars roll in until they were interrupted by Mrs. Moore from the hotel who'd come in through the other door. "I have customers who'd like some clothes, Casey," the woman said, mildly irritated until she saw what they were looking at.

"Oh my lord," she gasped when she saw the cars, "I'd better get back to the hotel and tell Mr. Moore we're gonna need more tea cakes and more tea."

Casey followed her to greet the customers who were visiting Steampunk Society members from Arizona and had seen the dress forms on the porch the afternoon before when they'd arrived but had been too tired to venture out of their perfectly period hotel room and stayed in to experience a buffalo steak dinner in the dining room.

"My husband didn't want to come this weekend," one of the women said, "but, boy, he doesn't know what he's missing."

Casey smiled. "Well, take lots of pictures so you can show him and make him jealous," she said.

"Oh, we intend to," the other woman said with an impish grin as she picked up a set of pantaloons and checked the tag for the price. "One hundred percent cotton?" she asked as she tested a seam.

"Pre-washed before cutting and sewing right here in this building, and I also have the same done up in handkerchief weight linen, "Casey assured her. "It's a bit more expensive but cooler than cotton."

"Oh lord, yes," she said, rolling her eyes, "let me see that linen." Casey loved it when she ran across a customer who understood fabrics.

"Love your polonaise," the other woman said. "Such a versatile garment, though that one is somewhat set for this holiday and maybe Labor Day."

Casey smiled. "I'm already putting an order in for velvets for the Christmas season," she said. "Mr. Riley is planning a huge Cowboy Christmas event."

"Do you know which weekend yet?" the first woman asked, "because I think I'd like to make reservations at the hotel for that event now before we head back to Phoenix."

"I'm not certain," Casey said, "but if you stop back in later today or tomorrow, I'll find out and let you know."

"Thank you," she said, "and I'll take this whole underpinning kit. You can simply never have too many bloomers, especially in heat like this. I've half a mind to go back to the hotel and change into this beautiful linen now."

The other woman began to finger the delicate underthings and smiled. "You may as well ring me up a set as well in small."

By the time they began lining up for the parade through town, Casey had emptied most of her rental rack and was down to only a few sizes of petticoats and bloomers. She hated the thought, but she'd be sewing into the night to restock for the next day, hopeful it would be as productive as today.

"How's it going?" Tucker asked when he hurried into the kitchen for a beer out of the refrigerator. "Looks like half your girls are naked out front," he said with a chuckle.

"Yah, I was gonna redress them during the parade. How's it going everywhere else?" she asked.

"Great as far as I can tell. Even sour old Mr. Cooper had a smile on his face."

"Probably used one of those knives of his to cut somebody's throat and start his day," Casey mumbled as she took the cold beer from Tucker and swallowed some of it. She'd been talking and explaining pieces of garb to people all morning, and she was parched.

"The beer guys seem happy, the Pepsi guy looked covered up, and the Buffalo Grill was turning out the patties as fast as the poor guy could shovel 'em onto the buns," Tucker said with a broad smile.

"Oh," she said before kissing him, "the two women from the Arizona Steampunk Society want to book rooms at the hotel for the Christmas event and wanted to know the dates."

Tucker dropped down onto the futon. "You've got to be kidding me—Christmas?"

"You're the one who wanted an event to impress," Casey said with a broad grin. "They're impressed and want more."

Tucker took out his phone and scrolled through his

calendar. "How does the second weekend in December sound?"

Casey nodded. "Far enough from Thanksgiving and not overly close to Christmas that you could get folks out. Keep the advertising local and tout it as a family event where people can come and do their Christmas shopping, enjoy an intimate meal at the hotel, and join in Christmas caroling with the gals from the dancehall the way they used to end the Christmas shows on *The Drifter* every year."

Tucker hugged her. "Aw, Dad would love that."

"Then you'd better get down to the hotel and spring this Christmas thing on Mr. and Mrs. Moore while they're in a good mood."

"Good idea," he said and kissed her again. "I'll be back to watch the parade with you in a few minutes."

☙ 18 ❧

Tucker was overwhelmed with their success thus far and hoped it would continue through the rest of the long weekend.

"How are things going here at the hotel, Mrs. Moore?" he asked the woman who slouched on a stool behind the front desk.

"Trying to get three chambermaids in period costume to sweep the carpet with one of those old push sweepers is like herding cats," she said. "All they do is whine that the work is too hard, the dresses and aprons uncomfortable, and that there's no air conditioning."

"This is supposed to be 1876," Tucker said with a chuckle. "Tell them to stand beneath one of the ceiling fans. Maybe that would help."

"No, because then I'd have three lazy girls standing under a ceiling fan, and my customers' beds wouldn't be getting made or the carpets swept."

"I just wanted to let you and Mr. Moore know that we've decided to put on a Christmas event the second weekend in December," he said. "I heard your Steampunk visitors from Phoenix wanted to book the weekend already."

Mrs. Moore rolled her eyes. "Then the silly girls will be whining that it's too darn cold."

"You should talk to that Haney fellow from Yucca about putting gas logs in all your fireplaces," Tucker told her.

"I'll pretty up a nice sign and post it here by the register, Tucker," Mrs. Moore said, "and thank you."

"Have you sold a lot of buffalo steaks and burgers yet?" he asked with a hopeful grin.

Mrs. Moore rolled her eyes and nodded. "Mr. Moore was reluctant to open the grills yesterday, but Casey came around and said there'd likely be good business, so we opened one and were overwhelmed immediately." She smiled. "I don't think Mr. Moore will be reluctant to take Casey's suggestions anymore."

"Me neither," Tucker said with a wink and a grin as he left the hotel to return to Miss Millie's and join Casey on the porch for the upcoming parade.

He pecked her cheek as she was putting a new calico dress on one of her wooden mannequins. He fingered the soft blue fabric dotted with sprays of white flowers. "This is pretty," he said and took the opportunity to study the outfit she had on. "And you look stunning," he said and smiled. "I guess it's the reason you asked for the additional buntings."

She twirled. "I made good use of them, don't you think?"

"I certainly do," he said and kissed her again. "I gather sales have been good already this morning."

Casey rolled her eyes. "I fear I'll be at my machine late into the night tonight so I have things to sell tomorrow."

"Is that good or bad?" he asked with an impish grin.

They heard trumpets blare from the cavalry outpost and then drumming from the Native American camp. "Sounds like the parade is getting ready to start," Tucker said. "I hope Mom and Dad are doing all right. They're leading everybody in a horse-drawn buggy Chris and Tandy fixed up for them."

"How was your mom's mental state this morning?" Casey asked as she fitted a skirt on the final mannequin and readied a lace-trimmed polonaise to go on over it.

"Pretty good actually," Tucker told her. "She called me Tucker and not Morgan, so that was a good sign."

Casey smiled. "Unless, of course, she saw you in those clothes and thought they were on set again."

Tucker's face fell. "I'd never even thought of it that way," he said. "She just seemed to be more like her old self again, and that was nice."

"Take the good days while you're still getting them," Casey said and kissed his cheek, "because the day will come when there are more bad ones than good."

"That's what I'm afraid of," he said as they watched the parade begin to move with trumpets sounding and drums pounding.

They saw Morgan and Rita in the carriage and Tandy on horseback in one of her new riding outfits.

As they waved, both Casey and Tucker caught sight of a bright auburn head and shoulders covered in garnet and gold silk. "Is that Charity in the polonaise I made for your mom to wear tonight?"

Tucker tried to follow the flashes of dark red hair through the crowd. "I think it is," he said, "but how in the name of heaven did she get mom's clothes?"

Tucker fished his phone out of his pocket and punched in a number.

"Hello," a male voice answered.

"I'm trying to reach Lupe," Tucker said, immediately worried for the old housekeeper.

"This is Manny, Tucker," the male voice said with nervous hesitation.

"Is everything OK?"

"Not really," Manuel Rodriguez said, "we're at the hospital in Rancho Mirage."

"What the hell happened, Manny? Is Lupe all right?"

"She said Miss Charity and her boyfriend came to the house, and she let her in though Mr. Morgan said not to anymore," Manny said, protective of his mother and her job with the Riley family, "but she thought it would be all right since Miss Rita and Mr. Morgan weren't home and Charity said she just needed to collect a few things she left in her room."

"But?" Tucker said, knowing there would be a but if his sister was involved.

"I guess one of them hit her on the back of the head," Manny said, "and when Mama came to, they'd ransacked the house, gone through Miss Rita's jewelry box, and," he said with a long pause. "And emptied the safe in Mr. Morgan's study."

"Holy shit," Tucker cursed. "How is your mom?"

"The doctor here says she has a concussion, but with some rest, she'll be fine in a few days if there's no bleeding inside her skull."

"I'm so sorry, Manny. Did she call the police?" Tucker asked as his eyes found Charity staring at him across the dusty trail with a mindless grin on her face like the cat that had eaten the canary.

"A lady at the hospital did," Manny said, "but she didn't give them much information because she was slipping in and out of consciousness."

Tucker was certain the old housekeeper had been

feigning her bouts of consciousness because she didn't know what her employer would want her to say regarding his daughter. "Tell your mom how sorry I am she got caught up in this shit with Charity and not to worry. She's done absolutely nothing wrong, and if the police are still around, she should tell them everything." He took Casey's hand and tugged her into the building to travel to the porch on the other end.

"What's going on, Tucker?" Casey asked as Tucker dialed the sheriff's office.

"I want to report a robbery and assault," he said and then launched into the information he knew. "The thieves are here at Desert Home," he said, "and I'll do my best to detain them until you can get officers here to take them into custody. They are Charity Riley and Jacob Miller, who both have open bench warrants now for missing a court appearance." Tucker listened as the person on the other end of the line cautioned him to be wary lest the persons in question were carrying firearms. "I'll be careful," he said, "but please get someone out here as soon as possible. We're having our Grand Opening event, and there are hundreds of people here."

"Tucker?" Casey asked as they saw Charity moving closer in the crowd along with the parade.

"I'm gonna call Chris for a little help," he said and put the phone back to his ear. A few minutes later, Chris came jogging through the crowd. "Where is the bitch?" he demanded to know. "She's gone too damned far this time."

Tucker watched Morgan and Rita pass, smiling and waving, blissfully unaware of what had happened in their home. The two brothers stood in wait for their sister and grabbed her and Jacob by both arms to drag them closer to Miss Millie's to wait for the Sheriff's officers.

"What are you doing in Mom's clothes?" Tucker demanded.

Charity glanced over at Mandy and her camera crew, who were walking over with ice cream cones in their hands. "Well, I had to have something to wear since you gave my clothes to that cheap tart over there."

Mandy was close enough to hear Charity's words and glowered at her. She leaned in to whisper to her sound man. "Can you get audio from that bitch this far away?"

He took something from his pack and grinned. "Oh, yah, boss," he said. "We can get every word out of that big mouth of hers."

"Cool," Mandy said, "let's hold back and act like we're getting filler from the crowd while we stay riveted on her and Tucker. I think it's his sister Charity, and from what I've heard, there's been bad blood between them of late."

Bobby grinned. "Then this could be some really good stuff if we can get it."

"Let's shadow them, shall we?" Mandy said.

"What happened at the house today, Charity?" Tucker demanded. "Are you the one who hit Lupe, or was it your boy toy Jake who whacked a poor old lady on the head and then ransacked our parents' house and ripped them off like a common thief?"

"Who told you that bullshit, Tucker?" Charity demanded. "You know that lying old Mex has always had it in for me."

"You mean since you had her son busted for supposedly raping you?"

Charity shrugged her shoulders. "So, maybe I raped him first," she said flippantly, "but the silly boy wouldn't leave it alone when I wasn't interested anymore, so he deserved what he got."

Chris snorted. "Two years in juvie?"

"Even Daddy said he should have gotten at least five years for what he did to me," Charity said.

"But he didn't do anything to you, Charity," Tucker hissed at his sister. "You had Manny thrown in juvie for two years just to feed your damned ego and get attention from everyone."

"Of course," she sneered, "you never bought it, did you, brother?"

"Only because I know you, sis, and I've been listening to your bullshit lies for decades."

Charity smiled. "It's because I'm so good at it, and why nobody will believe that old Mex when a pretty white woman is telling her story."

"You're a liar and a thief, Charity," Chris said in disgust. "Lupe and Manny are family, and you treated them like crap."

Two sheriff's deputies approached them. "Are you Tucker Riley?" one of the men asked.

"I am," Tucker said, "and this is my brother Christopher."

"And these other two?" the other deputy asked.

"Charity Riley, and Jacob Miller, the fugitives I called about," Tucker said. "There is a bench warrant on record for them because they missed a court date, but now they've broken into my parents' home, robbed it, and assaulted their housekeeper Lupe Martinez, who is in the hospital in Rancho Mirage now."

"It's all lies," Charity said. "The old Mex and her son are out to get me because he raped me and went to jail for it when I was in high school." Charity smiled at Tucker "Well, you know how the damned Mexes are," she said, batting her eyes and glancing up at the deputy.

"No, ma'am, I really wouldn't," the dark-skinned Hispanic deputy said to Charity, who took a step away from the man, "but after spending twenty years on patrol in Hollywood, I'm very familiar with entitled rich bitch celebrity types who think they are the be-all end-all of humanity and to hell with everyone else."

Chris chuckled. "Sounds like he knows you, Sis."

"We'll take them from here, Mr. Riley," the Hispanic deputy said as his partner cuffed Jacob behind his back.

"Before you cuff her," Tucker said and unbuttoned the polonaise before pushing it off Charity's shoulders. "Mom is supposed to wear this tonight," he said, "and not you."

"I'd suggest you search their car to look for the things stolen from my parents' home," Chris said. "It's mostly movie and television memorabilia, but also some cash and bonds from their safe."

Tucker's phone rang. "Hello, Mr. Tucker," Lupe said in a weak voice that broke his heart. "I am so sorry for allowing Miss Charity into the house, but I thought it would be all right because Miss Rita wasn't at home for her to harass."

"It's all right, Lupe. You didn't do anything wrong, and she's in custody now."

"Mr. Tucker, you must ask her about the pills."

"What pills, Lupe?"

"When I go to get Miss Rita's pills at the pharmacy last week," Lupe said, "they were pink and not white like the ones Miss Charity has been bringing home every month for her. I ask Mr. Randy at the pharmacy, and he tell me the pills Miss Rita is supposed to be taking are pink and not white, so ask her about the pills, Mr. Tucker."

"I will, Lupe, and thank you," Tucker said. "Now, just relax and get better so you can come home to us." He disconnected and turned to his sister, who stood between the deputies with Jacob. "Tell me about the pills, Charity?"

Tucker demanded and lunged at his sister. "Tell me about the pills you've been giving to Mom."

Charity smiled at her brother. "That was a real prize when I came across that article," she said with a giggle. "It seems there's a medication in Mexico they used to treat schizophrenia that actually induced dementia, so they stopped using it and distributed it to little *farmacias* in places like San Felipe and Tia Juana and asked few questions when someone came asking for them."

"Why would you do that to our mother?" Chris demanded. "That woman gave you everything you ever wanted."

Charity snorted. "We were trapped here in Desert Home," she snapped. "We were on set while they were filming, and otherwise, we were on excursions to hospitals with those damned horses to show what devoted parents Tucker and Charity were and how much they cared about the sick children of their fans," she spat. "It was disgusting, and I hated every minute of being a part of it." Charity spat on the ground at Tucker's feet. "And then they came up with this," she said, motioning around Desert Home, "and Daddy put me here to help you make it work."

"Which you had no intention of doing," Tucker said in surprise at her venom.

"This damned place can burn to the ground as far as I'm concerned, and then the ashes plowed into the sand," she spat with her eyes narrowed.

"And have you been giving that shit to Daddy?" Chris asked.

Charity smiled. "I added one or two to every bottle of Southern Comfort he brought home," she said. "I figured he'd be in about the same condition as the bitch in a year, and then we could commit the both of them, sell the ranch, dump this place, and finally be free of them and *The Drifter* once and for all."

The big Hispanic deputy tugged on Charity's arm. "Let's go," he said. The other took control of Jacob. "I'll tell my commanding officer that attempted murder should be added to the counts against this one," he said, nodding at Charity,

Mandy walked up, glaring at Charity and made certain her cameraman got a good view of her without the Polonaise and the petticoat yanked up above her breasts. "Now who looks like the cheap tart?" she hissed, "especially with those nice silvery bracelets on your wrists."

She turned to Tucker. "I have plenty of evidence you can use against that bitch," she said, "and I'll send it to you as soon we have it processed."

"Thank you, Mandy," Tucker said. "I really appreciate it."

"It's been an amazing event, Tucker," Mandy said. "Let us know when you plan to have another," she said, tugging at the old Charity costume, "but I'd probably rather have something made by Miss Casey the next time."

"You got it, Mandy. Keep your calendar open for our Christmas event the second weekend in December," he said.

Mandy gleamed. "I can just see all the velvets and satin now."

19

At five o'clock, when the cavalry sounded the end of the day's festivities, Casey was beat, and her shop looked like a carcass picked over by vultures. As people returned their day-use rental costumes, Casey threw them in the washer to process them for the following day.

"Are you going to shower and change before the big dinner tonight?" Tucker asked, looking exhausted in his dusty clothes. "Mom and Dad have been resting in my fifth-wheel for the past couple of hours. I think they both passed out as soon as they got out of their clothes."

"Do they know about Lupe yet?" Casey asked as she unbuttoned her polonaise and took off her bonnet. "I think I'll just wash the dust off in the sink," she said. "I don't want to get my hair wet."

"I told Dad everything, and he seemed to understand. Tucker wrapped his arms around Casey and pulled her close. "This really would have been unbearable without you here."

Casey smiled and ran a hand over his stubbled cheek. "I didn't do anything," she said, "and you need a shave."

"I suppose I should bring a few things over here," he said with a soft chuckle before kissing her again. "Would Miss Millie be scandalized if I did?"

"Miss Millie, yes, but Casey, not at all."

"Did you make something new and beautiful to wear tonight?" he asked.

"I made this," she said, motioning to her red, white, and blue ensemble, "but it is dusty and sweaty now."

"Wear the black one with all the little white ribbon," he said with a grin. "That's my favorite anyway."

Casey kissed his cheek. "Anything for you, my love." She went to her trunk and lifted out the black taffeta polonaise and flounced white petticoat. "Should I go over to the fifth-wheel and help your mom get dressed?"

Tucker shook his head. "No, Tandy is taking care of that tonight."

"I hope she recovers quickly after she gets back on her correct medication."

"Chris and I ran into Randy, the pharmacist from town, and he said she should snap out of it almost immediately once she's back on the pink pills and off the white ones. He told me the pharmaceutical names for each drug, but my brain is in no shape to put that shit to memory yet."

"Do you have a gate count yet?" Casey asked. "I'm sure everyone at dinner will want to know."

Tucker smiled. "Sixty-six thousand adults," he said. "Can you believe it?" He shook his head. "Only in my deepest imagination did I hope for that many folks coming out to see our little place here."

"Let's pray we get as many tomorrow or that at least everybody tells their friends," Casey said with a sigh.

"Hey," he said, "we sold over twenty-thousand two-day passes today."

Casey brushed out her hair. "That's pretty impressive for a first-time event." She heard her washer chime and went in to throw the clothes into the dryer. When she returned, she found Tucker fast asleep on the bed. She smiled as she ran hot water into her washbasin from the shower. She spent twenty minutes washing the sweat and dust from her body and then pulled on the petticoat and polonaise she'd be wearing that evening.

She shook Tucker awake. "You'd better wake up, cowboy, and go home and change for supper."

Tucker's eyes fluttered open. "With you here," he said groggily, "this feels like home."

Casey kissed him. "That's such a sweet thing for you to say. Are you happy with the way things went today?" she asked. "I mean other than the whole mess with your sister and all."

Tucker rubbed his eyes. "I really don't see how it could have gone any better. The parade went off without a hitch, and none of the Indians scalped any of the cavalry in their sleep last night." He grinned. "And how did it go for you compared to your fair experiences."

Casey rolled her eyes. "I've got to say I'm impressed, and I'm gonna have to be up late tonight sewing to give my racks the impression of being full."

"Didn't you count your till?" he asked.

"Oh, yah," she said, "and that's impressive as well, but I'm not going to jinx things by throwing around numbers until after the closing bell tomorrow."

"It's a long weekend, so the encampments won't be clearing out until Monday."

"Yah, but like fair guilds, those folks do their buying on the first day, and I won't see any of them on Monday except in passing." She smiled. They make their major purchases first and then spend the rest of their cash on food and drink for the weekend."

Tucker sat up and kissed her. "You have this thing pretty much figured out, don't you?"

"It's not all that different from what I was doing before except in a permanent structure rather than a canvas tent."

"From what I could tell, the girls across the way were kicking ass and taking names in your canvas tent."

Casey smiled. "I'm just glad I could help. Poor Wren was so stressed over everything."

Tucker stood up. "Well, I'd better get going and get Mom and Dad lined out for supper."

"I hope Mr. Moore still has some of those buffalo steaks," Casey said, "because I'm so hungry I think I could eat the whole buffalo."

"I think the steaks and the burgers were a real hit," Tucker said, "but I'm not certain what they're serving tonight. Might be the regular rubber chicken we get at the monthly meetings."

"At this point, I'd eat about anything so long as it was hot and not the texture of shoe leather."

He kissed her again. "See you in a few." He left through the door at the store end of the building.

Casey followed his tired gait toward the RV area and gazed up Front Street to see it had cleared of most of the stragglers. The Gingham Kitchen was closed up tight, and only a few lights shone in the storefronts. From experience, Casey knew everyone was exhausted, and she had the experience. For the majority of these merchants, this was their first time working an event like this one. With sixty-six thousand through the gate in one day, they'd gotten a workout. She couldn't wait to talk to Wren and Tandy to get their opinions on the day.

She switched off the lights in the store and returned to the bedroom to put on her makeup. Her stomach growled, and she thought about making herself a bagel. She pinned her bonnet on instead and headed for the Dancehall and the table reserved for her and the Riley clan near the raised dais. For the first time, she wondered where Sue was and hoped the woman hadn't fallen back into her old ways and found a bottle of gin.

Wren and her girls walked in dressed in Calico and smiled when they saw Casey sitting alone at the table. Eddie and the older girls found their table as Wren came over with a broad smile on her face and Ellie holding her hand to join Casey.

"So, what was all of that with Charity and the cops earlier?" Wren asked with concern and curiosity on her face.

"Mean Charity whacked some old lady and put her in the hospital," Ellie said as she climbed into a chair beside Casey, "so the police took her to jail."

Casey grinned. "And the seven-year-old-grapevine beats me out again."

Wren stared from her daughter to Casey. "She really put some lady in the hospital?"

"Morgan and Rita's housekeeper," Casey said in a hushed tone, "but I'll give you the details later unless Miss Ellie here already knows what they are."

Wren smiled and nodded. "How were your sales today?"

"Great," Casey told her, "and yours?"

"Ice cream beat out general merchandise two to one," Ellie said in a matter-of-fact tone, "but costume rentals and sales were very good."

Wren frowned at her daughter, but Casey smiled. "My sales were better than rentals," she said, "but I've got to do ironing after I eat so I have something presentable to rent tomorrow too."

"Yah," Wren said, "I've got stuff in the washer and dryer too."

"And it's a good thing I had extra stuff cut out because I'm gonna have to sew tonight so my racks don't look completely bare tomorrow."

"Well, I don't know about everyone else in the Merchants' Association, but we're happy as hell," Wren said with a bright smile.

"Watch that language, Mother, or I'll need to get the soap." Ellie cautioned.

"Go over and join your father and sisters, young lady," Wren said sternly. "I hope they're going to serve this dinner early so I can get her home and in bed."

One of the dancehall girls came around and took their drink orders, and Casey told her the others would be joining her soon."

"I'll join my crew as soon as she brings me my drink," Wren said. "Are these things always this exhausting?"

"Only the very best ones," Casey assured her as the doors opened and the Rileys entered the building to loud applause. "Well, I suppose that answers the question about how good everybody's day was."

The girl brought Wren her sloe-gin fizz, and she stood to join her family at the other table. Casey sipped her Jack Daniels and Coke as everyone took their seats except Tucker, who mounted the dais and tapped on the microphone to make certain it was working.

"Good evening, everybody," he said with a broad smile on his face. "I hope you all did well today." There was more applause, along with whistles and cheers. "Our gate count today was sixty-six thousand," he said, "and twenty-four thousand of those purchased two-day passes, so we'll have that many at least back again tomorrow." He raised his hands to quiet the cheering. "Our resident expert in this sort of thing, our Miss Millie, Casey Miller, tells me those are outstanding numbers for a first-time event, and I have to agree. Please stand, Casey, and share these accolades with me because without your valuable input, it never would have happened."

Casey stood with her face red and accepted the applause. She sat after a few minutes and Tucker continued. "We've decided to have a Christmas Event the second weekend in December," he said, "so we'll swap out ice cream for hot chocolate and hot cider and maybe turkey legs rather than buffalo burgers, but it's still several months away with plenty of time for planning. "I've also been approached by the SASS folks about setting up monthly shooting events here and by some of the other groups about holding events here as well. I think Desert Home is on its way, folks," he said with a bright smile.

Casey watched Morgan squeeze his wife's hand. "This is just what we wanted, Mother, and our boy has made it happen for us the way he said he would."

"She's looking a little agitated," Tandy whispered in Casey's ear. "I hope they bring the food soon."

"Does she know what happened at the house yet?"

Tandy shook her head. "Chris went over there and said it's a terrible mess, so we're going over in the morning to try and clean it up before Tucker brings them home."

Casey nodded. "Probably a good idea. I'd offer to go with you, but I'm the only one in the store."

"At least we have Sue to help us out," Tandy said. "The woman is so good with the kids and the horses."

"I wondered where she'd gotten off to," Casey said with a relieved sigh. "What all do you guys have set up over there, and how did you do moneywise today?"

"For five bucks, a parent can leave their kid for up to two hours," Tandy said, "and we have a petting zoo, the pony rides, and the miniature horse carts for the younger kids. For the older ones, I set up a little range like the cops use in their training with cut-outs of a lady with a baby, a gnarly bad guy with a revolver, and a raging bull, or cute little calf." She smiled. "It's all about teaching them to be observant and know what their situation is when they have a firearm in their hand." She shrugged. "I do a little trick shooting and give them some target practice with the laser shots, not live rounds."

"Probably a good idea," Casey said with a grin.

Tandy snorted. "Half the little gang-banger wannabees would probably be shooting one another." She laughed. "Chris wanted me to give them paintball guns, but I told him he would have to be the one doing the laundry when they shot me and got paint all over my clothes."

"Speaking of clothes," she said, "how are the ones I made for you working out?"

"Perfect," she said. "they're comfortable, easy to get in and out of, and wash up really nice."

"Good," Casey said. "I'm glad to hear it."

"I noticed a couple of gals walking around in some today. You must have made some sales."

"It was a really good day," Casey said. "If tomorrow is half as good, I'll be thrilled."

"You think we'll be doing something this big again anytime soon?"

Casey shrugged. "I know he wants to do the Christmas thing in December," she said. "Maybe Labor Day? I don't know. He doesn't want to overload the market with too many weekends, but if we start getting bookings with these roleplaying groups then," she shrugged. "who knows?"

"This would be a great location for one of the big

national SASS events," Tandy said, "and I think the folks you invited from the national organization are pretty impressed."

"I think the Tribes are talking about a Powwow too," Casey said. "Tucker is really jazzed about it all."

"Do you think the dancehall would be a good place for a wedding reception?" Tandy asked with her cheeks turning pink.

"I think it would be the perfect place for a wedding reception," Casey said, excited for her friend. "Did he ask?"

"This afternoon," she said, holding up her left hand to display a diamond ring.

"It's beautiful, Tandy," Casey said, wrapping her arms around her friend's neck. "I'm making your dress, of course."

Tandy smiled. "Of course, you are."

Tucker had been talking again, but Casey hadn't been listening until sour old Mr. Cooper stood. "It would really have been nice if somebody had told us there were going to be this many people here, so we could have been better prepared for the volume of buyers."

Casey couldn't help herself and began to laugh. Tandy joined her, and soon the room was laughing uproariously at the absurdity of the man's comment.

"Well," Tucker said with a wink at Casey, "I'd say that's my cue to return to my seat. Thank you all for hanging in there with me and helping to make this dream come true for my parents, my brother, and me. You'll never know how much we appreciate each and every one of you who joined us in this crazy venture and as we move forward, we hope you all prosper."

Tucker returned to Casey's side as the salad was being served. Buffalo roast followed in brown gravy with carrots, potatoes, and biscuits. For dessert was hot apple pie with vanilla ice cream, and by the time the final cup of coffee was poured, Casey's eyes were drooping.

"I'm going to need a few more cups of this," she said, "because I have a ton of work to do yet."

"Make it at home," Tucker told her. "I'm going to go help Tandy and Chris get Mom and Dad settled into the fifth-wheel for the night, and then we're gonna take one last stroll around the site to make certain the Indians aren't scalping the cavalry. Then I'll be in to help with what I can."

Casey smiled. "That would be great, baby," she said and kissed his cheek. "Did you see the ring Chris gave Tandy?"

"What?" he said with his eyes wide.

"Yep," she said with a broad grin. "It looks like the next big Christmas event here at Desert Home is going to be a wedding."

20

As Casey ironed the final skirt from her basket of rental garb, she heard the door to Miss Millie's opening and someone stepping softly inside. "Is that you, Sue?" she called out but was shocked to see the snarling male figure striding toward her with a tire iron in his hand.

"What the hell are you doing here, Michael?"

"I just came from seeing my brother," he stormed, "and he's been denied bail."

"He's been denied bail because he didn't show up at his last court date and because he put a poor woman in the hospital with a concussion, Michael. Jacob being denied bail is nobody's fault but Jacob's or maybe his girlfriend Charity's."

"That's a lie, Casey," Michael snarled. "Jacob wouldn't hurt a fly."

"Well, there's a woman in the hospital in Rancho Mirage who'd beg to differ," Casey said, never taking her eye off the tire iron in her former husband's hand.

He gazed around the building. "I can't believe you gave up our beautiful home to come out here and live in this damned shack just to play at more costume bullshit, Casey," Michael stormed.

"I'm not playing at anything, Michael. This is my business," she yelled, "and as you know full well, and it's a very good business."

"I don't know shit," he spat.

"Yah, well, you never seemed to mind spending the cash I brought home, and there was plenty of it for you to spend as I recall."

"You're still the same lying bitch you always were, Casey."

Casey's mouth fell open. "I'm tired of this, Michael," she yelled and pointed to the door. "Now get out of here so I can get back to work."

"Work my ass," he yelled. "What's this one's name? Jacob told me you're screwing the son of some has-been old actor."

"Who I screw is no business of yours anymore. Especially not since you took up with some bimbo from your firm's secretarial pool." Casey tightened her grip on the handle of the steam iron. "We're divorced now, thank the lord."

Michael raised the tire iron, and Casey raised the steam iron, pushing the button to release hot steam as the tire iron came down on her head and shoulders. Michael screamed, and Casey grunted as she lost consciousness.

"Lying bitch," Michael snarled as he stared down at his bleeding former wife. He grabbed her arm and began to drag her into the tiny bedroom off the living room. He shook his head again. "How can you bear to live in such a hovel after what you had in Santa Clarita with me? What I'd given you!" He tossed the tire iron on the floor and dropped Casey's arm. "Let your worthless lover find you on the floor like the filthy piece of trash you are, Casey," Michael hissed as he went to the fireplace and turned on the gas. He then moved to the stove and turned it on as well. "Let the damned gas take you and be damned with you once and for all."

Michael was about to deliver a kick to Casey's head when someone hit him with something, and he withered to the floor.

Sue found her phone in her jeans and punched in Tucker's number. "Some guy has hurt Casey," Sue screamed into the phone when Tucker answered. "No, I don't know who it is, but he beat her with a tire iron or something and the building is full of gas." She listened to Tucker for a minute. "OK, OK," Sue breathed into the phone. "I'm turning off the gas and opening the doors and windows now."

Casey woke with someone calling her name and urgently patting her cheeks. "Casey, baby, can you hear me?" Tucker pled. "Can you hear me, honey?" he asked when her eyes fluttered open.

She grabbed his wrist. "If you don't stop smacking my face," she muttered groggily, "I'm gonna get up and kick your ass. It hurts my head when you do that."

The high-pitched wailing of the ambulance siren cut through her skull like the sharp edge of Mr. Cooper's blades through one of the buffalo steaks in the hotel's restaurant. Casey squeezed her eyes shut against the pain. "Does anyone have an aspirin?" she asked. "Or a shot of morphine maybe? My head is killing me."

"And she's back," Tucker said with a sigh of relief as they bundled Casey onto a gurney and strapped her down for the trip to the hospital in Rancho Mirage.

"It was Michael," Casey whispered as the ambulance made its way over the bumpy road through the high desert until it found smoother running on the blacktop near Yucca and picked up speed.

At Eisenhower Hospital, Casey was admitted to intensive care and put into a private room before X-rays of her head and torso were taken and she finally received pain medication that sent her into blissful, pain-free sleep.

Casey woke next to find Sue beside her bed. "I need to get up and get out of here," Casey said when her eyes finally focused. "I've got sewing to do, or I'm not going to have stock for the booth tomorrow."

Sue took her hand and smiled. "Sweetie, tomorrow was three days ago, and you had plenty of stock."

Casey furrowed her brow in confusion, but it hurt. "Three days?"

"It's Wednesday, and you've been out like a light," Sue told her.

"Wednesday?" Casey gasped. "I missed the final day of the opening?"

"Slept right through the whole damned thing," Sue chuckled.

"How'd it go?" Casey mumbled. "Was Tucker happy?"

"Tucker will be very happy now that your eyes are open and you're not talking gibberish any longer," Tucker said as he bent and kissed her bandaged forehead.

"How did the event turn out?" she asked him. "What were the numbers on Sunday?" Questions came out of her mouth faster than she could process them. "Were the vendors happy?"

"Hush, Casey," Tucker said, trying to quiet her. "The doctor said you're supposed to be resting while that hard skull of yours mends."

Casey closed her eyes and drifted back into a peaceful slumber. When she woke again, a nurse was taking blood and the room was dark and quiet. She could see stars in the night sky outside her window and asked for a drink of water.

"Well, it's about time," Wren said when Casey woke again. "Everyone's been worried as hell about you, Miss Millie."

Casey grinned. "Where is Tucker?"

"He, Chris, and Tandy took Morgan and Rita back home today," she said with a giggle. "I think they were all getting a little stir-crazy cooped up in that camper together."

"I can imagine," Casey said with a deep sigh. "How was Sunday, Wren? Nobody will give me a straight answer when I ask. Was it a big bust or something?"

Wren smiled. "You really missed a great day, Casey. The gate was over fifty thousand, I think, and we ran out of ice cream about one, and I had to send Eddie into town for more."

"Oh, thank god," Casey breathed before her eyes snapped open. "What about Miss Millie's?" she asked. "I never got a chance to sew that night before …" Her voice trailed off, remembering Michael's red, angry face coming toward her with the tire iron raised over his head.

"Miss Millie's had an excellent day," Wren told her. "When Sue came over and told us what happened with your ex, Livie told Sarah and Ellie they'd have to run the Gingham Kitchen and went right over and took your place. She said you'd been showing her how to sew, merchandise the store, and run the register while she was over there helping with the bonnets and hat pins."

Casey smiled. "She's a smart kid and picks things up quickly.

"She absolutely loves decorating those little hats," Wren said, "and making those stick pins to keep them on a woman's head." She smiled. "Anyhow, she just planted herself in Miss Millie's for the night, finished up that ironing, and set up the rental rack for the next day. Then she dressed the mannequins and spent Sunday taking care of business."

"Please tell her how much I appreciate her help," Casey said. "I've told her before that I'd pay her a ten percent commission on any sales she made if she ever wanted to come to work for me," Casey said with an embarrassed glance at the girl's mother. "Not that I was trying to steal your help away from the mercantile or anything like that."

"Yah, right," Wren said with a giggle. "Well, at a ten percent commission, I think you just paid for my little girl's first semester in college." She took a printer tape from her register and handed it to Casey. "You're gonna be busy when you get out of here," she said, "because I think most of those are for orders already paid in full."

"What?" Casey gasped when she saw the day's total at the bottom of the tape.

"Livie said the two of you had been talking about putting together some complete packages to dress a woman from the underpinnings to the hats, and I think she ran with that idea and sold several of those packages."

"Damn," Casey sighed. "Now I know I'm gonna have to steal your best employee, Wren."

"That's all right," the woman said with a shrug, "my other two girls and their father have already told me they're moving the Gingham Kitchen into the back of the mercantile or building a building to house it in the lot next door so they don't have to work out of the tent anymore and can add a soda fountain and maybe hot drinks to the menu. They've all been listening to you preach marketing," she said with a faux frown. "Now I need you to start preaching laundry." Both women laughed, and Casey thought it was nice to have another friend.

"Did you see the ring Chris gave Tandy?" Casey asked.

Wren rolled her eyes and nodded. "That's one hell of a rock." She lifted her hand. "Makes my poor little thing look like a damned chip." She tipped up her soda can and swallowed. "I wonder if they've set a date yet."

"It'll likely be soon," Casey said. "Tandy's never been one for long drawn out engagements, and I'm certain they're gonna do it at Desert Home and make an event of it. I'd bet at the Christmas event."

Wren took out her laptop. "You've gotta see this," she said. "I recorded it at the Association dinner we had on Monday afternoon."

She booted up the machine, pressed some keys, and Morgan Riley came into focus on the screen. "I want, on behalf of my family, to thank all of you for helping us to make this dream of Desert Home come true." He seemed clearer than Casey could remember ever seeing him and thought the effects of the poison Charity had been feeding him had cleared his system. "Back in 1955 when the producers first came up with the idea of *The Drifter*, the studio found this old, abandoned town out in the Owens Valley, dismantled it, board by board, and transported it here to become our set." He nodded and smiled. "That's right, this old dance hall was a dance hall long before you or I ever stepped foot in it, and the hotel hosted guests before televisions had ever been thought of." He sipped water from a glass on the podium. "Now you have all breathed life back into these old buildings and back into Desert Home." He brushed a tear from his eye, "Rita and I thank you from the bottoms of our hearts."

Wren turned off the laptop. "I had no idea my store

had been anything more than a television prop before, did you?"

Casey shook her head. "Not a clue," she said, "but I intend to do some research and find out as much as I possibly can. Wasn't the Owens Valley where they made Western movies back in the day?"

Wren rolled her eyes. "Yah, after ol' Mullhulland sucked all the water out of it to send to LA back in the thirties and forties," she said. "I think there are still families trying to get reparations for that. It was lush farmland filled with orchards and such," she said in disgust, "and he just raped it because he could in the name of progress and the mighty Los Angeles."

Casey shook her head. "That's really sad."

"Sad but true," Wren said, "and if our little town here came from there, then it might make a really good human-interest story for Mandy down at the television station. She's trying to work herself off the weather platform and onto the news desk, you know."

Casey smiled. "The exposé of Charity she did to help get Manny's record expunged for that supposed rape was a huge step in that direction," she said.

"Then I say we put our heads together and see what we can ferret out about this old town," Wren said.

Tucker walked in. "And just what sort of trouble are you two cooking up now?" he asked as he walked over and planted a kiss on her forehead.

"What do you know about the old town that Desert Home used to be over in the Owens Valley?" Casey asked. "Wren and I thought it might be something to investigate for future promotional material."

Tucker shrugged. "That's something you'd need to talk to Dad about or look in the paperwork we got from the studio when we bought the property," he said.

Lupe, who was also in an intensive care room, saw Tucker and came shuffling in, dragging her IV pole along with her. "How is Miss Rita, Mr. Tucker?" the old housekeeper asked respectfully. Is she better now with the pink pills?"

Tucker helped Lupe to sit and kissed the top of the older woman's graying head. "She's much better, Lupe, thanks to you."

"I do nothing, Mr. Tucker but tell you about the pills," Lupe said with her face turning red.

"And because of that," he said, "we found out the truth."

Lupe shook her head. "I still can't believe what an evil girl that Miss Charity is," she said. "First, she steal my Manny from me for two years with her lies, and then she try to steal her mama's mind for greed."

"How is Manny doing, Lupe?" Tucker asked. "Did he call that attorney I suggested?"

Lupe smiled. "He did, Mr. Tucker, and the man tell him he can expect a big settlement from the state for wrongful imprisonment for listening to Miss Charity's lies and not investigating the way they should have."

"And how are you feeling, Lupe?" Casey asked, touching the tender spot at her temple. "I'll sure be glad when this headache of mine finally goes away."

"The doctor says I go home tomorrow," Lupe said with a nervous glance at Tucker, "but he say not to go back to work for two weeks."

Tucker nodded. "Don't worry about that," he said. "Chris, Tandy, and I have that covered, and with Mom's meds straightened out, she's almost back to her old self again."

"I'm so glad to hear that, Mr. Tucker," she said as she rose from the chair on unsteady legs. "I better get back to my room now before that *bruja* nurse come looking for me with her evil needles." They all laughed as Tucker escorted Lupe back to her room.

"Well," Wren said, getting to her feet as well. "I'd better be getting back up the mountain as well before my crew decides to build an addition onto the place."

21

After Mandy did a segment about the town of Worthy in the Owens Valley, the Moores received a visit from a very special gentleman.

Mrs. Moore was surprised one Wednesday afternoon when an old man in his advanced years came through the door of the hotel. A younger man followed him with old photo albums filling his arms. The men stared around the lobby for a few minutes and then settled into the Eastlake sofa in front of the fireplace, the older gentleman with tears streaming down his age-spotted face.

"May I be of assistance, sir?" Mrs. Moore asked, going to his side.

The old man opened one of the albums with trembling hands and handed her a tin-type photo. "Does anything look familiar to you, madam?"

Mrs. Moore studied the old black and white photo, moving it closer to her eyes. "This looks like my lobby," she said as her eyes went from the fireplace in the photo to the one just beyond the sofa.

The old man smiled as he used his sleeve to brush tears

from his cheek. "That's because it is," he said. "When my great-grandfather opened this hotel in 1859, it was called the Worthy Arms." He turned a page to show her the portrait of a distinguished couple seated before the fireplace. "My grandparents," he said, "Russell and Virginia Worthy after my grandpa settled in the Owens Valley from Illinois." He offered her his hand. "I'm Russell Worthy the third, and this is my son Russell Worthy the fourth," he said, "and I never thought I'd ever see this place in reality." He took a linen handkerchief from his pocket and blew his nose. "Aside from the photos in these albums and the stories my Grandma Ginny told me as a kid, I thought this place was just something made up from her imagination."

"You never saw it as a child?" Mrs. Moore asked. "From what I understand, they didn't move it here until the fifties for the filming of *The Drifter*."

Mr. Worthy shook his bald head with a fringe of thinning gray hair around his elongated ears. "The area dried up after Mulholland stole the water for LA," he said with a frown, "and everyone moved away from the valley and Worthy." He glanced at his son and smiled. "We moved to San Bernardino when I was nine or ten and by then the town had been purchased by the movie company to use as a set in their Westerns with stars like Tom Mix and Talula Bankhead." He smiled at Mrs. Moore. "I saw the news feature about Worthy and how it had been moved all those years ago and couldn't believe it. I just had to come and see it for myself, so I had Rus drive me up here."

Mrs. Moore smiled. "Please let me get you gentleman a room, sir, and be our guests here in Desert Home for the night while you visit the remade town. I know we'd all love to see your photos of Worthy as it was all those years ago and hear any stories you have to tell us."

"You're actually using this as a functioning hotel for guests?" his son said with his eyes wide.

"Absolutely," she said, "and I've put a lot of time and effort into making the rooms as close to period as I could imagine. Would you happened to have photos in those books that show the rooms the way they were while the hotel was still open in Worthy?"

He handed her the stack of albums. "The hotel and the rest of the town as well," he said.

Mrs. Moore settled the old man and his son into a downstairs room and then got on the phone with Wren, Casey, and Tucker to tell them about Russell Worthy and his amazing albums. Casey called Mandy and the reporter arrived in time for supper with everyone and the man in the Buffalo Grill which he told them had been called 'The Worthy Room' back in the day. He showed them photos of the restaurant with taxidermized heads of elk, bear, and buffalo on the walls.

"Here's one of Grandma Gin at the door of the saloon," he said with his cheeks flushing red, "but she couldn't go in there anymore since she was now a respectable married woman with children." He grinned. "You see, Gran worked there as a dancer before she married Grandpa Worthy."

Casey went through the albums slowly, studying the clothes the women wore in the photos. "This is an absolute goldmine of fashion history, sir," she said enthusiastically. "Would you mind if I made photocopies of these?"

"Not at all, young lady," he said. "My Gran's sister Clementine actually ran a dress shop in Worthy." He flipped through the pages until he came to one and showed it to her.

The breath caught in Casey's throat when she recognized Miss Millie's in the old black and white photo with Clementine's stenciled on the sign above the porch where Miss Millie's sign now hung.

She showed it to Tucker and he smiled. "I guess they tried to repurpose the buildings as close to their original uses as possible," he said. "It's something you should point out to Mandy when she does her follow-up feature about Worthy with all this amazing new information."

Mr. Worthy wept again when Casey pointed out Miss Millie's to him and told him she ran the dressmaker's shop now that had been his great aunt's all those years ago.

"I barely remember my Aunt Clementine," he said, "but my Gran loved her and thought she was a pioneering woman to run her own business when that just wasn't done by women at the time."

Everyone gathered to tell Mr. Worthy good-bye the next morning. "I think you've all done Worthy proud," he said, "and I can't wait to tell the family they were actually seeing it every week on television back when they watched *The Drifter*." He gazed up and down Front Street. "I remember Gran saying how Old Man Mulholland had come in and stolen the water from the Owens Valley and then the movie studio had come and stolen the whole damned town, but what you folks are doing here is a wondrous thing, bringing it all back to life again as Desert Home."

The evening after the wedding Casey sat with Tucker in front of the fire. "I can't believe this is actually where a woman named Clementine lived and worked doing the very same thing I do now," she said as she stared at the stacks of cut fabric on the table waiting for her attention. "I'd almost be inclined to repaint my sign and be Clementine rather than Millie," she said with a nervous grin.

Tucker kissed her. "Do you think Clementine would be more inclined toward scandalous behavior than Miss Millie?"

"Well, she did have a sister who worked in the dance hall," Cassey reminded him, "and she dared to be an independent businesswoman when business was considered the exclusive realm of men."

"Very true and very scandalous, indeed," Tucker said with an impish grin on his face. "Why don't we go to bed and you can let me decide whether I prefer Miss Millie or Miss Clementine."

The wedding of Chris and Tandy ended up the main feature of the Cowboy Christmas weekend. The ceremony was held in the little church that doubled as the community schoolhouse and was beautiful, decorated with green pine garlands and white poinsettias.

The bride wore ivory velvet, taffeta, and lace while the groom and his brother, the best man, wore period waistcoats in black silk and brand-new Stetsons.

Rita Riley wore a gown made from kelly-green velvet trimmed in red satin for the season, and her husband wore much the same as his sons. Casey stood as her friend's matron of honor in green and red plaid with a red poinsettia fascinator in her hair, accented with small green ostrich feathers artfully designed by Livie in place of leaves.

Mr. Moore's Buffalo Grill catered the reception held in the dancehall and presided over by Miss Millie's grown-up niece Patty, whom Morgan had introduced some weeks before at a monthly Merchants' Association dinner. Most folks in Desert Home hadn't known Sue had been the young actress who's played the part of the precocious child Patty back in the fifties and accepted her readily as the new proprietress of Charity's Dancehall and Saloon.

She purchased her franchise with the money she made expanding the hotel to include twelve additional rooms on three floors for the Moores and finishing ten additional cabins for Tucker in the east pasture. Desert home was growing by leaps and bounds.

.

"Charity's Dancehall and Saloon" was now Patty's and all the employees wore much more comfortable attire designed and sewn by Casey.

A cheer rang out as the bride and groom kissed and the pastor introduced Mr. and Mrs. Christopher Riley to the guests.

Tucker and Casey followed the beaming couple from the church hand-in-hand. "You look lovely in that plaid, Casey," Tucker whispered to her, "but what sort of wedding dress would the dressmaker sew for herself if she were the one getting married?"

Casey glanced up at the handsome man by her side. "If that was supposed to be a proposal, Mr. Riley, it was pretty lame."

Tucker's face paled. "No, ma'am, not a proposal, just a simple question."

Casey grinned at his discomfort. "I sew for others every day," she said. "If I were getting married, I'd buy a dress and not make one for myself."

Tandy turned around with a grin on her face. "Don't let her kid you, Tucker. All she talked about while she was making mine was what she'd make for herself if she were the one getting married, and she has plans for a different dress for every season."

"And that really was a lame proposal, Bro," Chris added, laughing.

"I'll keep that in mind should the occasion ever present

itself," Tucker said, tripping on a small rock as they marched toward the dancehall for the reception.

"Looks like Clementine's has business," Tandy said as they marched by.

"Livie is quite capable of handling it," Casey said but studied the crowd none-the-less to see what might be transpiring.

Two women carried boxes down the steps, and Casey thought she recognized them as her Steampunk customers from the opening weekend. They hurried to the street with their phones out, snapping photos of the wedding party, and all the women stepped forward to have their photos taken.

"Mrs. Moore, Sue, and I are putting together some wedding packages for gowns, rooms, and grub," Casey told Tucker, "and we're going to start advertising them online to make Desert Home a wedding venue destination."

Tucker chuckled. "Well, you gals have managed to pull off miracles already in Desert Home, so I don't see why a wedding business should be any different."

Mandy and her crew were in attendance and got a great shot of Casey catching Tandy's bouquet of ivory and red roses.

"You're in trouble now, Bro," Chris teased his brother at their table set up on the dais.

Rita giggled. "There's no need to buy the cow if you're already getting the milk for free," she said in a tone reminiscent of her daughter Charity.

"Mother," Morgan said in a scolding tone to his wife. "Tucker would be lucky to have a woman like Casey as his wife."

Casey and Tandy returned to their seats as the music began to play. Chris took his bride's hand. "I think that's us, sweetheart," he said, and they went to the floor and opened the dancing.

Tucker offered Casey his hand as well. "Would you care to join the happy couple while the music is something I can still keep up with?"

Casey took his hand. "That's probably a good idea," she said with a smile.

They returned three songs later after Tandy and Casey had done a very provocative dance to a Stevie Ray Vaughan tune that had everyone in the dancehall laughing and clapping.

Chris elbowed his brother in the side. "Man, I think you'd better grab her while you can because I just saw old man Cooper giving her the eye with ill-intent if I've ever seen it."

The dancing and revelry went on until close to midnight when Chris and Tandy retired to the bridal suite at the hotel. Tucker escorted Casey back to her home where she put the bouquet of roses into a Mason Jar filled with water and checked by the register for Livie's totals for the day.

"I swear that girl could sell ice to Eskimos," Casey said when she saw the number at the bottom of the paper. "Looks like I'm gonna have to break out the brass gears, copper tubing, and top hats too. Liv says the Steampunk Society is booking their Spring get-together here."

Tucker nodded. "Yep, just signed all the paperwork yesterday and sent it off."

"I'm gonna have to get some Edwardian stuff cut out and some felt bowler hats and top hats for Liv to decorate before then."

Tucker grinned. "Wren is going to be stealing her back from you someday, you know."

Casey smiled. "Not as long as what I'm paying her is

filling up her college fund. How many kids her age do you know who are raking in a grand on a weekend like this?"

Tucker lifted a brow. "Sounds like I should be working for you," he said and kissed her softly on the lips.

"If you could sell dresses the way Livie does," Casey giggled, "you would be."

22

Tucker tossed and turned uncomfortably beside Casey that night. Did she want him to ask her to marry him? He loved spending time with her and he certainly enjoyed the time they spent together in bed, but did he want to be married again? Did he love her enough to make her his wife? Hell, did she even love him? They'd never talked about how they felt about one another. If she loved him, wouldn't she have said it already?

"What's the matter, sweetie?" Casey asked after he'd elbowed her in the side for the tenth time.

"Just can't seem to get my brain to shut up tonight," he said. "Sorry if I'm keeping you awake."

Casey rolled onto her back. "What's the matter, Tucker? You only toss and turn like this when something is really bothering you."

Tucker rolled his eyes mentally. Was he really that easy to figure out? "Do you want to get married, Casey?" he finally blurted into the darkness.

She snorted a soft laugh. "That's a pretty lame proposal too, sweetheart," she said. When he didn't say anything, she continued. "Are you serious, Tucker? Where is this coming from all of a sudden?"

"I just thought with Chris and Tandy tying the knot, you might have that in mind as well," he said propping himself up on one elbow. "I mean it sounded like you'd been talking to Tandy about dresses and all."

"I'm a seamstress, Tucker," she said in irritation. "I talk to my friends about dresses a lot, and the subject of wedding dresses has been at the top of the discussion list for several weeks now with Tandy's wedding and all the discussions about putting wedding packages together for the venue here at Desert Home."

"Oh," he said and exhaled. "I suppose that makes sense."

"My last husband just tried to bash my head in with a tire iron," she said, "so I don't think I'm in any hurry to put myself in that situation again anytime soon."

Tucker put a hand on Casey's belly. "I hope you know I'd never do anything like that to you, Casey."

"I never thought Michael would have either," she snorted, "so what does that say about my judgment when it comes to men?"

Tucker rolled over to stare at Casey. "I've treated you with nothing but respect, Casey," Tucker said, "even when you threw yourself at me like a whore in your bed."

Casey's mouth dropped open in shock. "I think it might be a good idea if you got out of my sinful bed now, Mr. Riley, and went home to your own."

"Fine," Tucker said and jumped from the bed, grabbing for his trousers. "Thanks for nothing, Mrs. Miller," he called as he stormed out of the bedroom and eventually the building.

Tucker stopped halfway back to his fifth-wheel. Why had he said something so stupid? Was he that afraid of getting married again? She hadn't deserved that, and Tucker was ashamed of the words as soon as they'd come from his mouth. Should he go back and apologize? Instead, he trudged on to his camper, undressed, and went to bed after swallowing a cold beer.

The following morning he and Casey were supposed to meet Tandy and Chris in the hotel's restaurant set up in Patty's for breakfast before the couple left for their honeymoon in San Diego. When Tucker entered the hotel restaurant Casey was sitting beside Tandy with her eyes red from weeping. He bypassed the table for his office and slammed the door behind him.

"Was that an icy breeze I just felt blow through here," Chris said as his eyes followed his brother to the office and flinched when the door slammed.

Casey got to her feet and rushed to the restroom with tears streaming down her face.

"I'd better go and see what's going on here," Tandy said and followed Casey to the restroom.

Chris stood and turned toward the office. "Yah, I guess I'd better do the same," he said and went to the office..

"What the hell's going on here, Tucker?" Chris asked as he watched his brother pouring Jack into a glass. "Why are you drinking your damned breakfast when you've got a day of work ahead of you with the cars lining up at the gate already?"

Tucker threw back the glass of liquor and swallowed. "Casey and I split last night."

Chris's mouth fell open. "What the hell happened, Bro? I thought things were good with the two of you?"

Tucker glanced up at his brother. "I may have called her a whore," he said, filled with embarrassment.

"You're an ass, Tucker. How could you have talked to her like that?"

In the restroom, Tandy put her arms around Casey. "What happened, Sweetie?"

Casey wiped her eyes with a wet paper towel. "Tucker asked me last night if I wanted to get married," she said. "It wasn't a proposal or anything like that."

Tandy snorted. "Yah, cause he's so good at that."

"No," Casey said, "he just wanted to know if I wanted to get married again, and I told him no because my last husband had just tried to kill me with a tire iron and I really didn't trust my judgment in men much anymore."

"I can certainly understand that," Tandy said. "So what happened to cause all the trouble between the two of you?"

Casey wiped her eyes again and began to sob. "He called me a whore for taking him to bed."

Tandy's eyes went wide with rage. "He called you what?" She turned on her heel to hurry out of the restroom, stormed to the office, pushed open the door, and marched up to face Tucker. "You called her a whore?" she hissed before drawing back and slapping Tucker hard on the face. "You're an unmitigated ass, Tucker Riley. Do you have any idea how hard she's been working to get that Steampunk event here?" Tandy said. "And that Powwow from the Morongo tribe? I hope you don't think either of those just fell into your lap because you have such a pretty face," she hissed.

Tucker's eyes went to the door just in case Casey had followed Tandy and stood outside the office door. "She was just doing it to put money in her register like any good whore," Tucker said, regretting his words again. His mother had always said he needed a throttle governor between his brain and his mouth sometimes. Tandy slapped him again with much more force than the last one.

"Now that was uncalled for, Tucker," Chris said in a scolding tone.

"I'm sorry," he told Tandy. "It was a long night, and I didn't get much sleep."

"Well, I hope you don't think she did either," Tandy snapped as she took her husband's hand. "Let's get out of here. I can't bear looking at this ass for another minute, and he's made me miss my breakfast." Tandy scowled up at her new brother-in-law. "You know how much I hate flying on an empty stomach."

Tucker watched the bride and groom leave the building, then he trudged off to the restroom as well. His long face with circles beneath his eyes stared back at him in the mirror as he washed his hands. "I can hardly bear to look at myself either," he muttered at the man staring back in the mirror. How had he let this happen and lost the best thing that had happened to him in years?

Cars filled the parking lots as they had on the opening, and Tucker's vendors appeared to be happy with the crowd and the sales when he checked in on them throughout the day—all except one, and he gave her shop a wide berth. No sense kicking an already riled hornet's nest.

Three months after Christmas, Tucker stared up from his desk to see the glowering faces of Wren, Mrs. Moore, and Sue staring down at him. He suspected that even on her honeymoon, Tandy had contacted the women and filled them in on what had happened between him and Casey on the night of her wedding, and he could only imagine what had gone on since. Tandy and he had made a concerted effort to avoid one another since the couple had returned to Desert Home from San Diego.

"I don't suppose you've seen this," Wren said as she

opened her laptop, punched some keys, and set it down before him on the desk. A full-screen shot of Casey's shop came into view with the words, ESTABLISHED HISTORICAL CLOTHING FRANCHISE FOR SALE superimposed over it.

"Livie and I both tried to ask her about it," Wren said with concern in her voice, "but all we got was that she thought she needed a change of scenery."

Tucker stared speechless at the computer screen. Was she really going to sell out and leave Desert Home?

"We've finally got this thing dialed in, Tucker," Mrs. Moore said, "and we can't afford to lose Casey and all her good marketing ideas. What the hell happened, and why haven't you fixed it yet?"

Tucker cleared his throat. "It was a personal matter between the lady and me," was all he said.

"Well," Sue snorted, "we think you need to get this damned personal matter sorted before we're all out of business here in Desert Home."

He slammed his pen and white-knuckled fist onto the desk. "And maybe it's time Desert Home stood on its own two feet and stopped relying on Mrs. Miller to see it through. Isn't that what you organized your Merchant's Association for in the first place?"

"Now you just sound like your sister, Tucker," Sue scolded her younger cousin. "No matter how badly you've gotten your feelings hurt, Desert Home and her merchants need Casey Miller and her input here. She's also the reason a good number of people come back to Desert Home for every event. They want to see what she has new in that shop." Her tone softened. "And I think you need her too," Sue said with a deep sigh, "no matter how much you hate to admit it to yourself or anybody else, Tucker."

All the women stared down at him as they might a little

boy who'd just fallen and skinned his knee doing a silly stunt on his bicycle. Had he been moping around all that much since Casey had thrown him out of her bed?

"What does the Merchants' Association have planned for the Steampunk weekend?" Tucker asked in an effort to change the subject.

Wren finally smiled if reluctantly. "We've really been pushing the balloon rides," she said. "Did you get a close up look at that thing when they brought it out here for Mandy and her crew to film for the spot on the news?"

Tucker nodded. "It's really something, isn't it? I'm thinking I might even book one of those suites in the gondola for the weekend. They were small but ornate."

"Definitely something directly from the mind of Vern or Wells with all that shiny brass strapping holding the gondola in place," Wren agreed. "Rides in that fancy thing over the desert will be a big draw for the weekend."

"And they have their insurance certificates all lined out?" he asked. "Can't have them taking people a thousand feet into the air if they're not insured."

"I believe so," Wren replied, "but I think Casey has been dealing with them on that, so you'd need to check with her."

Tucker nodded. "I'm certain she has it all well in hand." Casey was detail-oriented if nothing else, and Tucker could depend on her to make certain the fancy Zeppelin styled after the ill-fated Hindenburg with its gondola decorated in the style of the Gilded Age had all the necessary paperwork to operate out of Desert Home for the Steampunk weekend.

As the Memorial Day weekend and the big Steampunk Event approached, with the Zeppelin niggling at his mind, Tucker stopped by Clementine's. Casey was at her sewing machine with stacks of pastel fabric folded upon the table waiting to be constructed into garments.

"Hi, Casey," he said softly so as not to startle her.

"Tucker?" she said, jerking her head up with what he thought was a flash of anger in her blue eyes. "What can I do for you?"

"I was talking to Wren today," he said, "and she said you were handling the paperwork for the big balloon our Steampunk friends are bringing over, and I just wanted to make certain that was all in order."

"Oh," she said almost sadly. "I think they still have a final inspection to go through with the California Civil Aeronautics Board, but after that, they'll get me their insurance certificate and we'll be good to go."

"That's good to know," he said. "Well, you look busy, so I'll let you get back to it."

She patted a pile of pastel fabric. "Livie and I are anticipating a busy weekend," she said.

Tucker smiled. "We can only hope,"

She stood when he turned to leave. "How have you been, Tucker?"

"Busy with some fishing trips booked in the cabins," he said, "and getting things lined out for the long weekend ahead." He took a deep breath. "And then there was the court case with Charity we had to go through with Mom and Dad," he said.

"How'd your mom do with that?"

"She's pretty much back to her old self and extremely pissed with Charity," he said, "but more for what she did to Lupe than for what she did to her and Dad." Tucker grinned. "I swear she'd like to take the flyswatter to her bare behind if she could." He sighed. "And then I always get keyed up before one of these weekends worrying about if we're going to get a big crowd so my merchants here in Desert Home will be happy."

Casey nodded. "I hear that. Livie and I have been working like crazy to get these pastels and some bonnets finished and trying to get stuff made for the new photos Mrs. Moore wants to feature in the wedding venue adds online."

"How's that coming along?" he asked.

"I think she has three booked for the holiday season and another for next spring."

Tucker smiled. "That's actually pretty impressive."

"I think she'll make a go of it," Casey said. "She loves weddings, and she loves Desert Home."

"And how about you?" he asked. "Do you still love Desert Home?"

Casey stared at him while she pondered his question. "I do, Mr. Riley. I love Desert Home and what you're trying to do here very much."

Tucker wanted to take her into his arms and ask her why she wanted to leave, but he couldn't quite bring himself to do it. If she wanted to sell out and leave, that was her choice. He smiled mentally, thinking she must not be getting many bites on that ad as she was still here.

❧ 23 ❧

The Steampunk weekend arrived, and Casey and Livie rushed to put the shop in order.

"Do you think we're going to be busy this weekend?" Livie asked as she put an Edwardian-inspired tulip skirt on one of the mannequins.

Casey shrugged. "This will be the first time we've ever had a chance to cater directly to the Steampunk crowd, and I'm a little nervous that we don't have enough of the Edwardian stuff and too much of the Western."

Livie added a bowler hat decorated with brass gears and feathers to the ensemble. "Well, Desert Home is a cowboy television set, so what would they expect?"

Casey dressed another mannequin in Edwardian underpinnings made from light-weight linen and decorated with lace and satin ribbon. "I know," she said, "but I still worry."

Livie smiled. "And that's what makes you so successful. Your customers know you care about what you present on their behalf."

Someone tapped on the door that neither one of them had unlocked yet. Casey rolled up the shade and saw Mandy on the porch with her crew dressed in vests and bowler hats. She opened the door, and they all pushed into the room. Mandy wore a bowler as well, but she had on a double-breasted trench coat dress made of dark blue poplin that fell to her ankles to show her lace-up boots.

"We wanted to stop in and see what you had to offer this weekend," Mandy said as she admired the bright red pinstriped tulip skirt ensemble on the mannequin. "This is adorable," she said, "but not really my color. Do you have it in blue by chance?"

Livie went directly to the rack and came away with one ensemble in light blue poplin and another in dark blue pinstripe silk taffeta. "These are both in your size if I remember correctly," Livie said, handing the reporter the more expensive silk to study.

Mandy smiled. "I adore this little tie-on bustle addition," she said as she looked at the price tag and grinned. "I'll take them both and wear the silk to the Grande Ball tonight."

When she saw the one-piece silk undergarment, she had to have them as well. Her film crew smiled as they watched her shop. By the time they left Clementine's, Mandy had added a top hat dressed with a hatband studded with brass gears and a split skirt with a matching double-breasted jacket.

"You can bet your ass she'll want to cut all of this," Bob the cameraman said, "but I'm gonna make sure the production editor down at the station cuts some of it in for shits and giggles." He chuckled before they left.

"Well," Livie said with a smile, "there's your first big sale for the day."

Casey rolled her eyes. "You mean your first commission and addition to your college fund."

Livie frowned as she returned from the kitchen with two cups of coffee. "Are you really going to sell this place, Casey? I just can't see anybody else caring as much about the store and its customers as you do."

Casey sipped the coffee as she looked for another dress for the empty mannequin she wanted to feature on the porch. She chose one of the new pastel polonaises they'd made from gingham and coordinating eyelet fabric and topped it with a French bonnet decorated with pastel corn husk roses and satin ribbon.

"I haven't sold it yet, have I?" Casey said. "I refuse to sell to someone who knows nothing about the period, the clothes they wore, or how to construct a garment."

Livie grinned. "That last lady who came to talk to you about buying seemed to know what she was talking about."

Casey snorted. "You mean the one who said I should have been using cheaper fabric and less lace on my polonaise to lift the profit margins and then went on to tell me I should only be selling bustles made from plastic?" She glanced at the grin on Livie's face and knew the girl was just trying to rile her about selling the franchise in Desert Home. "She also said your hats and bonnets were ridiculous and should be thrown in the dumpster."

"Is that why you didn't sell to her?" Livie asked with a grin. "I think it's actually because you're in love with Mr. Riley and don't want to go."

"You read too many of your mother's romance novels," Casey said, trying to suppress a grin. "Maybe I didn't sell to that puffed up know-it-all because I knew the quality in the shop would drop to imported cheap Chinese trash if I did."

"I don't think the Merchants' Association would let

that happen," Livie said. "I know Mom and some of the others are working on Association rules now to keep the quality of merchandise in the stores where things are supposed to be handmade up to par and guarantee they don't bring in imported junk from China and Korea."

"I'm glad to hear that," Casey said with a sigh. "It pissed me off when I saw made in China stamped on some of the stuff in Mr. Cooper's shop the other day."

"Mom too," Livie said, "and I think she read him the riot act over it and made him take them out."

Casey grinned as she topped another mannequin's head with a black top hat Livie had decorated with a silk scarf and large brass gear that accented the brass buttons on the double-breasted trench-coat dress. "I don't think this hat looks ridiculous at all," she said with a giggle as she moved the mannequin to the porch. "I think that's gonna do it," Casey said when she came back in. "Now we just have to wait for the parade and the customers."

"We didn't have as many in as I expected yesterday," Livie said.

"I don't think there are that many camping," Casey said. "I know the hotel is filled, all the cabins are rented, and I think I heard all the rooms in Yucca are taken. Maybe the bulk of those coming up are just day-tripping."

Livie giggled. "Maybe all the Steampunks are like Mandy and have to have four walls around them and a flush toilet for their fannies."

Casey giggled, thinking about the reporter who was always dressed to the nines trying to camp in a tent and sleep in a sleeping bag on the ground with only a porta-potty at her disposal to relieve herself. "No, I don't see all that silk finery in a porta-john. Do you?"

"Not hardly," Livie said with a giggle as they heard the

trumpets sounding the beginning of the parade and their day.

Men and women paraded by in bizarre attire far beyond anything Casey could have imagined with leather masks that resembled the plague masks worn by physicians in Europe in the fourteenth century to actual gas masks and scuba tanks on their backs.

"What's that supposed to mean?' Livie asked when one of the costumed individuals marched by. "I don't understand what they're going for with that?"

Casey shrugged. "It's probably something from a Steampunk novel or one of Jules Verne's stories," she said with a shrug. "The long-tailed waistcoat was period though and the spats over his shoes."

Livie shook her head and smiled. "I'm sure glad you're around to explain this stuff," she said, "because I still don't have a clue for the most part."

"Don't be silly," Casey told the girl. "You're a quick study and know almost as much as I do about fashions in the nineteenth century."

"Only because I have a great teacher," Livie said as she followed two ladies in jeans and t-shirts into the store.

Morgan Riley walked up the stairs and greeted Casey. "Looks like another good crowd," the aging man said. "I assume we have you to thank for this like the opening last summer."

"I had very little to do with this, sir, other than placing ads for Clementine's in some of the Steampunk newsletters around the country."

He sat down in one of the chairs and reached over to take Casey's hand. "I don't know exactly what happened between you and my son," he said, "but I wish you could find it in your heart to forgive him for whatever he did or said."

"Mr. Riley," Casey said, trying to stop the man.

"My boy is a good man," he said, ignoring Casey, "but like his father, if he doesn't have a script to go by, he can sound like an ass sometimes." He took a deep breath and continued on as Casey's face flushed with embarrassment. "He's done nothing but mope around since the two of you had your parting of the way," he said, "and his poor mother and I just want our boy back." He squeezed Casey's hand. "Please take him back and send him back to us, Miss Casey. His mother is distraught over it, and I fear she may have a relapse of her former condition if she doesn't see a change in him soon."

"Tucker and I rarely speak anymore, sir. He stays out of my way, and I try to do the same," she said, trying to ignore the pain in the old man's eyes as she spoke.

"So, if he stopped by, you'd speak to him?" Morgan asked hopefully.

"I would, sir," she told him, suspecting she'd be getting a visit from the man's son in the near future.

Morgan Riley kissed her hand and then her cheek. "Thank you, Miss Casey, you've given this old man hope for a new day, and I know his mother will be glad to know you'll at least consider giving the fool boy a second chance."

Two hours after her visit from Morgan Riley, Tucker walked into the busy shop. He walked behind the counter where Casey was ringing up a customer. "Dad said you wanted to talk to me," he said softly into her ear. Casey couldn't ignore the thrill it gave her to have him so close and smell his familiar aftershave.

Casey grinned. "I think it was more like he wanted you to talk to me," she said.

Tucker rolled his big brown eyes, and Casey saw his cheeks turning red. "I'm sorry, Casey. He had no right sticking his nose into our business, and I'll let him know how I feel about it too."

Casey grabbed his sleeve when he turned to leave. "Don't, Tucker," she pled. "Your mom and dad are just worried about you, is all."

"Both of them were at you?" he said in anger.

"No, it was just your dad, but he said your mom was concerned too, and he's afraid she might fall back into dementia, worrying about you."

"Christ," he spat as a customer approached the counter with her arms filled with garments.

"Will you wait for me out on the porch swing, and I'll be out as soon as I ring up this customer?"

"Sure," he said and stomped off through the living quarters to the front door.

Casey took the garments and began to write up a receipt.

"That man looks very familiar," she said, staring off toward where Tucker had gone through the curtain to her living quarters.

Casey smiled. "Did you ever watch *The Drifter*?" she asked.

"Oh my God," she gasped, putting her hand to her mouth. "That was Tucker Hughes?"

"The son of the actor who played him," she said, "Tucker Riley."

"I can't wait to get home and tell my dad I saw Tucker Hughes right here in Desert Home like on the show." She handed Casey the cash for her purchase, took the bags, and left the store.

Two more customers stood in line, and Livie was busy with another, so Casey dealt with them as well, answering questions about washing instructions and other general questions about the garments.

She saw Livie smiling, knowing Casey loved to educate customers about the history of a garment. "Thank you, ma'am," Casey said as the customer exited with her purchase, and Livie joined her behind the counter. "I've got to go out front and talk to Tucker," she said. "He's waiting for me on the porch."

"Go ahead," the girl said with a grin. "I've got it covered here."

"You're a good girl, Liv," Casey said and kissed her cheek, "and I'm pretty certain we've got the first semester of your Junior year covered after this weekend."

Livie grinned. "Get on out there and see what Tucker wants," she said. "You know he has no patience when it comes to waiting."

"I know," Casey said with a sigh and left the shop. She stopped at the refrigerator and grabbed two cold beers, and then joined Tucker on the porch swing. "I'm sorry that took so long," she said and offered Tucker the beer. "By the time I finished with her, there were more ladies in line, and Livie was covered up."

"I figured," he said as he popped the caps off the brews and handed one to her. "You're a handy guy to have around, Mr. Riley," she said and swallowed a mouthful of the cold beer. "Damn, that feels good on my parched throat."

"Been busy, I gather," he said with a broad smile.

"So far, most of the other merchants have been as well though Mr. Cooper was grumbling a bit."

Casey chuckled. "As if that's anything new. What's his problem today?"

Tucker stretch. "It seems nobody explained to him what a Steampunk is, and for some reason, he thought they were pirates and made a shitload of pirate-themed toys, yard art, and blades."

"I suppose we were supposed to educate him too," Casey snorted. "He's a grown man with a computer. He could have googled Steampunk or simply asked somebody if he was unsure."

Tucker nodded. "You'd have thought," he said, "but evidently not our dear Mr. Cooper."

Casey just shook her head and swallowed more beer.

"Are you attending the grande ball tonight?" Tucker asked.

"Are you kidding?" she said with a grin. "The place is going to be filled with women wearing my gowns. Of course, I'm going."

He took her hand. "Would you care for a handsome and dashing escort then?" He glanced at her smiling. "These Steampunk types would call themselves dashing, wouldn't they?"

Casey began to giggle. "Dashing always makes me think of the cartoon character Dudley Doright."

Soon they were both laughing. "Then you'll do me the honor of accompanying me to this shindig?"

"I'd be honored, sir," she said and offered him her hand. "And at what time will you be collecting me?"

"I believe the Ball starts at eight," he said hesitantly, "but I bought a weekend slot on that airship, and it includes dinner for two as they fly us over the area, and that leaves at six. Would you by chance be interested in that?"

Casey lifted the watch hanging from her waist and checked the time. "They should be sounding the get-your-asses-home trumpet soon, and I'll change into my new gown," she said as the trumpets blared to sound the end of the day. "That's it, I suppose," Casey said with a grin, "so I'd better go run my register and then change and freshen up."

Tucker stood. "Then, I shall be back to collect you in half an hour dressed in my finest attire." He gave her a gracious bow along with a quick peck on the cheek.

"I'm looking forward to it, sir," she said very formally as they walked back into the living quarters together.

24

Tucker didn't know why he was so excited, but he was as he walked across the street to the mercantile to check and see how Ed, Wren, and the girls had done that day and make arrangements for one final surprise for Casey tonight.

"Did you talk her into dinner in the gondola?" Wren asked with an excited look on her face.

"We're picking her up in half an hour," he said.

"Then we can all walk over together," she said. "This is as close to a date night as I've come to in ages, and I'm thrilled." She twirled around in her new gingham dress and smiled.

Ed took his wife's hand. "Now I feel like an absolute ass for not treating the best woman alive to a night out on the town before now."

"As well you should," Wren said with a giggle as they entered Clementine's, where Casey stood waiting in a gown of pewter silk embroidered in gold. "That is absolutely stunning," Wren gasped as she studied the gown.

"You don't think it's too much, do you?" Casey asked,

running her hands over the lines of the formfitting tulip skirt and ball gown bodice.

"You look like something from an old Mae West film," Wren said in admiration. "And here I am in gingham," she said, running her hands over the gingham and eyelet creation Casey had designed for her and that Livie had sewn.

"Don't be ridiculous, Sweetheart," Ed interrupted. "You look stunning as well."

Wren patted the hand of her mate. "Thanks for that, my love, but we both know you didn't get a beauty queen when you came home with me," she said with a soft giggle.

Tucker listened to the conversation around him but couldn't take his eyes off Casey. Wren had been correct. She stunned in the dress she'd chosen, and he wondered again how he'd gotten so lucky. He just hoped he hadn't completely blown it with her.

"The dress really is beautiful," he told her in a soft whisper.

"Thank you," she whispered in reply with her cheeks burning. "I thought Clementine should be a little daring for this dinner tonight."

Tucker chuckled. "You look perfect."

They made their way to the airship and were ushered inside by a dapper young man in a waistcoat and starched collar. Tucker had been staying in a room in the ornate gondola all week, but the opulence of the reimagined Gilded Age took his breath away every time he stepped inside the dining room. Crystal chandeliers hung from the ceilings, and polished brass gave the look of gold to most surfaces. Tucker could almost imagine Diamond Jim Brady and Molly Brown sitting in a corner together and smiled again when he glanced at Casey in the flamboyant dress.

"Oh my word," Wren gasped as they took seats in the

dining room. "I heard from Mrs. Moore that this place was fancy, but it's really over the top, isn't it?"

Tucker chuckled. "I'll take you to see my stateroom later," he said, "where I even have a gold toilet seat."

Casey's mouth dropped open. "You've got to be kidding, a gold toilet seat?"

"I don't care much about the toilet seats," Ed said. "I just hope the food is as good as at the Moores'. I'm in serious need of a good steak with all the trimmings." He studied the menu.

A master of ceremonies took over, and the Grande Gala got underway as the airship took off over the desert. Someone later told Tucker that the first sign of trouble came during the presentation of an award for best in show to Casey for her amazing gown and her dedication to the cosplay industry. Someone thought they heard the popping of a bolt as it sheered away from the gondola's brass struts that kept it rigid in the air. Tucker, caught up in the excitement of the moment, never heard anything but applause. The floor fell out from beneath their feet as the big airboat began its descent. The screams were unfathomable until they stopped, and there was nothing but unbearable silence over the desert again and the drone of the Zeppelin's big engines.

It was later determined that the weight capacity had been grossly exceeded by the operators of the ride, but that did nothing to ease Tucker's guilty feelings over the loss of life that night. Tucker hit the ground hard and must have blacked out as searing pain gripped his body. How far had he fallen, and where were his friends? Casey? Where was Casey? Tucker tried to call out her name but couldn't make the words come as he melded with the darkness around him and let the pain take him.

When he regained a sense of himself again, they were

putting him into an ambulance. Chris was there. "Casey?" he muttered, but all his brother did was shake his head as Tucker fell back into oblivion again.

"Tucker?" he heard his father calling, "It's time to wake up now, son."

Had he overslept for school again? The old man was gonna be pissed if he had. Tucker tried to move, but pain racked his body, and he remembered. His eyes flew open. "Where is Casey?" He demanded with fear edging his voice—fear of what they might tell him.

"Casey is fine, Tucker," Chris said. "She's at the mercantile with the girls."

"She's not hurt, then?"

"Broke her arm in the fall," Chris said, "but she'll be fine,"

Tucker knew his brother and could tell he was holding back. "What is it? What haven't you told me yet?"

Chris took a deep breath and glanced up at his father, who nodded. "It's Eddie and Wren," he said, gulping air to continue. "They didn't make it."

Tucker squeezed his eyes shut against the pain. "Oh dear God, those poor girls," he groaned with tears for his friends and their children streaming down his face.

Chris took his hand. "Dad is having the old Boot Hill Cemetery recognized by the county as an actual cemetery," he said softly, "and we're putting them there so they'll be closer to the girls."

Tucker narrowed his eyes. "I don't know that I want my friends a part of a tourist attraction, even in death."

"I know," Chris said sympathetically, "but they'll be in good company. Mom and Dad want to be buried there, too, when the time comes."

Tucker shook his head. "Isn't that taking this thing just

a little far? Do they expect us to put Tucker and Charity Hughes on the stones too?"

Tucker groaned when his brother made no reply. "Oh, good grief," he said and let his head fall back onto the pillow as the doctor walked into the room.

"How are you feeling, Mr. Riley?" the young man asked in a cheerful tone. "How is your pain today?"

Tucker glanced up at his brother. "I feel like I fell out of a damned Zeppelin," Tucker said without much humor behind the statement, "and my back is killing me."

"You suffered a serious sprain," the doctor said, "and I suspect you'll feel it for some time to come, but eventually, with some intense physical therapy, you'll find yourself back to a semblance of normal."

He had Tucker roll over onto his stomach, poked and prodded some, and then said, "I think we can release you in a day or two if we can get you up onto your feet and make certain your insides are working as they should concerning bowel movements and such." He grinned. "Someone from physical and occupational therapy will be up to see you soon to get all of that rolling."

Tucker rolled his eyes. He'd been through all of that before after a minor car accident. "Bring on your torture masters, Doc, I can take it."

The young doctor grinned. "Tell me that after your first session with our Miss Spivey."

Tucker spent three more days in the hospital before going home to his parents' ranch. It broke his heart that he had to miss the funeral of his friends, and he longed to see Casey to make certain she was all right after the harrowing night they'd experienced. Was she angry with him and blamed him for the loss of their friends? Tucker couldn't understand why she hadn't come to see him while he was in the hospital or after he'd been released.

He finally broke down and asked his brother. "Is Casey all right? I don't understand why she hasn't come around."

"She's been pretty wrapped up with the girls," Chris said. "It seems there were no relatives to take them in, and she's been fussing with the CPS people about getting custody or at least sharing custody with Liv, who is eighteen now and can legally take custody of her sisters."

Tucker swallowed hard. "I had no idea," he said. "Ed and I talked about a lot of things," Tucker said with a sigh, "but never about what to do in a case like this."

"And why would you?" Chris said. "It's not really a typical topic of conversation over a beer on a Saturday afternoon."

"I know," Tucker said, "but Eddie was my friend, and I feel like I should have at least known what he'd have wanted for his girls if something like this happened to him and Wren."

Chris snorted. "As if you could have known the bottom was going to fall out of that damned airship."

"I thank the lord everyday Mom and Dad decided to pass on the Gala that night," Tucker said.

"You and me too," Chris said with a nod, "you and me too."

Tucker took his brother's hand. "I'm glad you and Tandy weren't there either. I'd never have been able to forgive myself if something had happened to either of you."

Chris took a deep breath. "She was pissed at me that I didn't want to go because Casey had made her this killer dress to wear," he said, "but I think all is forgiven now."

Tucker smiled. "I should hope so, Bro," he said with a soft chuckle. "I should certainly hope so."

25

Casey woke confused in the hospital, unsure of where she was or what had happened until her vision focused, and she recognized Tandy in the chair across from her with eyes swollen and red from weeping.

"What's going on" she managed to croak out between parched lips. "My damned arm is killing me."

Tandy leaped to her feet and moved to the side of the hospital bed. "You broke it in the fall, sweetie, and they had to put a damned pin in it to hold it together," Tandy said with a forced smile, "but the doctor says you'll be good as new in no time at all and back at your sewing machine."

"Fall?" Casey muttered as her memory came slowly back. The screams of people who'd been sitting around her round her returned to pierce her skull. The vision of Wren's frightened face filled her mind as she grasped for her husband's hand before they fell away together into the darkness. "Wren?" she muttered, already fearing the worst.

The huge tears sliding down Tandy's face told Casey everything she needed to know. Her friend was dead. "She and Ed are both gone," Tandy told her

"And Tucker?" Casey asked, dreading the answer.

"He's alive," Tandy told her, "but Chris says his back is messed up some from the fall, and they're not sure he'll walk again."

Casey sighed with relief. At least he was alive. "The girls?" Casey gasped and grabbed for Tandy's arm. "Where are the girls?"

"Chris and I took them to the ranch until we could find a relative," Tandy told her, "but …"

"But what?" Casey demanded.

Tandy shrugged slightly. "There doesn't seem to be anybody. Both Wren and Ed's parents are gone, and neither of them had brothers or sisters that the girls know of."

Casey thought back on her many conversations with Wren and the subject of extended family had never come up. She knew Wren's parents had been lost in an auto accident when she was in high school and she'd spent several sad years in foster care, which she'd never want her children to suffer through.

"I guess CPS is searching for someone to take them in," Tandy said, "and plans to take them into custody once the funeral is over."

"Like hell, they will," Casey snarled. "Wren wouldn't want her girls in foster care after what she went through with touchy-feely foster fathers and rapist foster brothers. The girls will stay with me."

"Do you think you have it in you to take on three girls, Casey?"

"It would only be two," Casey corrected. "Livie is already eighteen and will be going off to college in the fall."

"I think you need to talk to her about that," Tandy said with a sigh.

"What do you mean?" Casey asked.

"I just think you should talk to the girls before you start making plans for their futures."

Casey was released the following day and was greeted at Clementine's by a somber crowd of fellow Desert Home merchants from the Association. "What are we going to do now, Casey?" Mr. Moore asked. "I don't see how Desert Home can survive the notoriety of this terrible disaster. The only people who'll want to come here now will be the looky-loos who'll want to see where the airship fell out of the sky and killed people."

Casey had to admit she'd been having the same thoughts. Bigger and more prestigious entertainment venues had been brought to heel after lesser disasters than theirs. "We're just going to have to put our heads together and think of something," was all she could think to say as she pushed her way into the peaceful comfort of Clementine's and made her way into the living quarters. "Home at last," she muttered to herself as she dropped onto the futon.

Later that afternoon Tandy brought the girls over for a tearful reunion. Ellie ran into her arms. "We don't want to be wards of the state," she wept.

"Mama always said that was a death sentence for girls like us," Sarah added. "She never really explained what she meant by that," the sixteen-year-old said, "but I can imagine."

"I'm eighteen now," Livie said defiantly, "and the state can't take you anywhere if I want you to stay with me right here in our home."

"Don't you girls worry about a thing," Casey said. "Between Livie and I, we'll work this out, and you can stay right here where you belong."

The day of the funeral was a somber one in Desert

Home. They held the service in the little church at the end of Front Street with all of Desert Home in attendance except for Tucker, who remained in the hospital. Ed went to his rest in a formal waistcoat, ostrich hide boots, and new Stetson while Wren wore a powder blue silk polonaise trimmed in bright white lace and a demure French bonnet on her head.

"You look so beautiful, Mama," Casey heard Livie whisper before they closed the coffin to carry to the cemetery.

At the rear of the little church, looking very much out of place in their mundane modern clothes, sat two women from CPS who pounced as soon as the graveside services had ended.

"We're here to take these minor children into custody," one of them said as the people of Desert Home, led by old Mr. Cooper, made a protective circle around the girls.

"These girls have a safe home right here with us," the old blacksmith snarled, "and you've got no right to take 'em if they don't want to go with ya."

The woman in a pink pantsuit reminiscent of Hilary Clinton stepped forward to go head-to-head with the old man.

"These children have no living relatives, and therefore, they have become wards of the State of California," she spat at the old man.

"I'm their living relative," Livie said, stepping forward, "and they're going to stay here at home with me where they belong."

The woman snorted. "And just how do you intend to provide for them, young lady?" the woman demanded, "by playing at cowboys and Indians up here in this ridiculous commune that got your parents killed in the first place?"

"Ma'am," Casey said with irritation oozing from her

voice, "Desert Home is neither a commune nor a cult, and we don't play at anything here. This is both our home and our place of business, which we're all very proud of, and if Olivia wants to keep her sisters here with her while she carries on what her parents were working so hard to achieve, then everyone here has her back." Casey narrowed her eyes. "And if you want to try us, then you can see just how much we've taken to heart that whole cowboy and Indian thing."

The woman's eyes went wide. "Are you threatening me?"

"Of course not," Casey said with her sweetest smile, "but Sarah and Ellie aren't going anywhere today or any other if their sister doesn't want them to go."

The other woman who'd remained silent up to that point spoke. "We'll see about that if we have to come back here with the sheriff and a court order to take them."

"You can try, lady," Mr. Cooper snarled and lifted one of his blacksmithing hammers to shake at her, "but you may find your ass in a sling if you do, and yes, that was a threat."

With that, both women scurried away to their county car, hopped in, and drove away. Ellie ran up to Mr. Cooper and hugged him while covering his face in sloppy, wet kisses. "Do you think we should take the girls to the ranch until all of this is settled?" Tandy asked Casey.

"Livie is their guardian," Casey said. "Where they go is up to her and nobody else."

In the end, the girls opted to stay at the mercantile with their sister and the rest of Desert Home watching over them.

Casey didn't see Tucker for another two weeks when he showed up at their regularly scheduled Merchants' Association potluck. He moved slower and used a cane to assist him when he walked.

When he saw her, he grinned. "Well, don't we look the pair," he said with a chuckle. "You with one wing and me down in my back."

"I'm sorry I never got down to the hospital to see you," she said, "but I had my hands full here with the girls and the funeral and all,"

Tucker shushed her with a kiss. "And I'm sorry I couldn't be here for that. Chris said it was nice, and you bid them a fine farewell."

Casey smiled sadly. "I wish I'd made her that dress to wear in life," she said.

Tucker kissed her head, grateful to feel her in his arms again. "She'll be wearing it for eternity now, and I'm sure she appreciates it."

Mrs. Moore, who'd assumed the office of president since Wren's passing, called the meeting to order. "Are we all in agreement that we should hold a grande reopening of Desert Home on the anniversary of last year's event?"

There was a good bit of back and forth about whether or not it was too soon after the tragedy until Livie stood and cleared her throat. "My mom and dad loved Desert Home and everything it stands for," she said, "and I don't think they'd want their passing in a freak accident to stop everything and everyone from moving forward with the dream of this place."

She returned to her seat, and the meeting went on with plans to bring back the media, more cosplay groups, and the Worthy family as special guests of the occasion.

At the end of the meeting, Tucker stood. "I can't begin to express how grateful I am to all of you for hanging in there with me and the family after everything that happened." He glanced over at Livie and her sisters. "We lost family and friends in that accident," he said, "and I'm proud that you all want to continue on this road with me."

He returned to his seat beside Casey, and she took his hand. "They all needed to hear that from you," she whispered into his ear, the smell of him strong in her nose. She hadn't realized how much she'd missed it—missed him until then, and it brought tears to her eyes. How many times since her breakup with Michael had she sworn off men? How many times since meeting Tucker? She shook her head. What was she doing here?

The meeting was breaking up, and Casey stood. "I guess I'd best be going," she said. "I'm glad to see you're doing all right, Tucker."

"Can we talk, Casey?" he asked, clutching her hand.

"I suppose," she said as he began to follow her back to Clementine's.

"Do you really think we can make this work after what happened?" he asked as they went up the stairs into Clementine's.

Casey turned to face him. "I don't see how we can't," she said. "There are too many people here counting on us to make it work, or they'll lose everything." She saw Wren's tear-stained face in her mind and resolved to give it her all just as she had before. This time she had a family to think of, and she didn't intend to let them down.

Tucker smiled and swept her into his arms, wincing with the pain in his back. "I may not be the man I was before the accident," he said, "but damn if I don't love you, woman." He kissed her hard, and Casey responded, twining her tongue around his.

She smiled to herself. "And I love you too, Mr. Riley."

EPILOGUE

The Grande Reopening of Desert Home, while attended by a good many of the aforementioned lookie-loos, was nonetheless a tremendous success for the Desert Home community.

"What would you say has been your biggest obstacle to overcome since the tragic incident?" the young reporter, who'd replaced Mandy Jewel after she'd been scooped up by a larger affiliate, asked Casey as she tended to her depleted rack of rental clothing.

"The loss of a very dear friend," Casey said in reply with a glance across Front Street to the mercantile where the Gingham Kitchen appeared to be doing a brisk business of ice cream in freshly made waffle cones.

People followed the parade of native dancers, gyrating saloon girls, and stiff-backed cavalrymen through the town, sampling the wares of the vendors along the way. Old Mr. Worthy led the parade in a jaunty carriage, wearing the top hat and tailcoat of the official mayor of Desert Home. The story of Worthy, California, was featured in the program handed out at the gate so everybody who cared to could read about the original town and what had transpired in the Owens Valley all those years ago to land the town in the place it rested today.

At the official dinner in the Worthy Room that night, the merchants of Desert Home sighed a collective sigh of relief as they thanked Tucker and Casey for a successful reopening of Desert Home and toasted to many more successful events in the months and years to come.

As they sat together hand-in-hand, Tucker bent and whispered something into Casey's ear. "Do you think you could top that beautiful dress you made for Tandy if some fool asked you to marry him in a proper fashion?"

When others around the room realized what was happening at the head table, they quieted as Tucker went to his knees. He brought a ring box from his jacket pocket, and Casey's eyes went wide in surprise. "Casey Miller," he said, clearing his throat in the eerily silent room, "Will you do me the honor of becoming my wife?"

When Casey didn't answer right away, Chris stood. "Oh, come on, Casey," he said with a nervous chuckle. "I've been coaching this bonehead on his speech for weeks now so he wouldn't say something foolish."

The crowd laughed at Chris and missed her reply completely as Casey wrapped her arms around Tucker's neck. "I'd be honored, Mr. Riley, but I'll likely buy myself a dress rather than make my own."

Tucker gave the thumbs-up sign and a cheer went up around the room, but Tucker knew the dress she'd marry him in would be one she designed and made herself with the assistance of her apprentice seamstress, Liv.

Dear reader,

We hope you enjoyed reading *The Return of the Drifter*. Please take a moment to leave a review, even if it's a short one. Your opinion is important to us.

Discover more books by Lori Beasley Bradley at https://www.nextchapter.pub/authors/lori-beasley-bradley

Want to know when one of our books is free or discounted? Join the newsletter at http://eepurl.com/bqqB3H

Best regards,

Lori Beasley Bradley and the Next Chapter Team

You might also like:
Tribal Law by Lori Beasley Bradley

To read the first chapter for free, please head to:
https://www.nextchapter.pub/books/tribal-law

Lightning Source UK Ltd.
Milton Keynes UK
UKHW021147271120
374179UK00003B/443